"There comes a time in a man's life when he thinks about what his legacy will be,"

Zane said. "When I die—"

"But that's a good many years from now!" Lesley tried interrupting.

"There'll be nothing in this world to say I've lived, that I've loved, that I cared. I have no family. No children. And I've come to realize those things are important."

Zane made his death sound imminent, and that distressed Lesley. She lowered her head.

"You want a child," Zane observed. "And I want an heir."

Lesley held her breath, then whispered the question. "What are you saying, Zane?"

"I'm asking you to marry me."

Dear Reader,

Silhouette Special Edition welcomes you to a new year filled with romance! Our Celebration 1000! continues in 1996, and where better to begin the new year than with Debbie Macomber's *Just Married*. Marriage and a baby await a mercenary in the latest tale from this bestselling author.

Next we have our HOLIDAY ELOPEMENTS title for the month, Lisa Jackson's *New Year's Daddy*, where a widowed single mom and a single dad benefit from a little matchmaking. Concluding this month is MORGAN'S MERCENARIES: LOVE AND DANGER. Lindsay McKenna brings her newest series to a close with *Morgan's Marriage*.

But wait, there's more—other favorites making an appearance in January include *Cody's Fiancée*, the latest in THE FAMILY WAY series from Gina Ferris Wilkins. And Sherryl Woods's book, *Natural Born Daddy*, is part of her brand-new series called AND BABY MAKES THREE, about the Adams men of Texas. Finally this month, don't miss a wonderful opposites-attract story from Susan Mallery, *The Bodyguard & Ms. Jones*.

Hope this New Year shapes up to be the best year ever! Enjoy this book and all the books to come!

Sincerely,

Tara Gavin
Senior Editor

Please address questions and book requests to:
Silhouette Reader Service
U.S.: 3010 Walden Ave., P.O. Box 1325, Buffalo, NY 14269
Canadian: P.O. Box 609, Fort Erie, Ont. L2A 5X3

Debbie Macomber

JUST MARRIED

Published by Silhouette Books
America's Publisher of Contemporary Romance

To Lillian Schauer, Attorney Extraordinaire.
Pam, Ruth and Wanda
This one's for you.

 SILHOUETTE BOOKS

ISBN 0-373-24003-1

JUST MARRIED

Books by Debbie Macomber

DEBBIE MACOMBER

hails from the state of Washington. As a busy wife and mother of four, she strives to keep her family healthy and happy. As the prolific author of dozens of best-selling romance novels, she strives to keep her readers happy with each new book she writes.

Dearest Readers,

I'll never forget that September day in 1982 when editor Mary Clare Kersten called to buy my first book. Those of you who know me personally will be shocked to learn I said five words the entire conversation: Hello. Yes. Thank you. Goodbye.

The sale of that first novel was the culmination of a dream I had nurtured and actively cultivated for four long years. Fourteen months later *Starlight* was on the shelves. It's fitting that my first published book was a Special Edition. Number 128.

Now Silhouette celebrates number 1000 with a lineup of writers that are some of the industry's finest. The editors have a right to be proud. Special Edition novels have touched the lives of women for 1000+ books and will continue to do so for many years.

I remember when I wrote *Starlight* and how I loved Rand, my blind hero, and Karen, the woman who became his light and his world. When my editor asked if I'd pen a story for this celebration, I wanted it to be one my readers couldn't put down. From page one I fell in love with Zane, the injured mercenary, and Lesley, the jilted bride, and I know you will, too.

As always, I'm pleased to hear from my readers. You can reach me at P.O. Box 1458, Port Orchard, WA 98366

Best wishes,

Debbie Macomber

Chapter One

Zane loved this old house. It represented everything that he'd never had as a child. Love. Warmth. Security. Happiness. The massive, three-story structure had once been in the family, but had been sold after the death of his grandfather fifteen years ago. Zane owned the house now, and he intended to make up for the years of neglect it had suffered.

He leaned against the support column on the wide veranda that circled the grand home. As it had in his childhood, the view of Lake Michigan mesmerized him, calming his spirit. There was peace here, something that had been sadly lacking in his life up to this point. He was a man who'd willingly involved himself in war, and over the years he'd been paid handsomely for his services.

Almost unconsciously, he rubbed the ache in his injured leg. The pain worsened as the day progressed, not that he minded the discomfort. It reminded him that he was alive and that two of his men, two of his friends, were not. It reminded him that he had yet to seek his vengeance.

Zane walked to the end of the porch, recalling his days as a child when he'd raced with careless abandon across the lush green lawn. There would be no more children chasing butterflies and dreams here. No children who would hide on the limbs of the maple tree and imitate the chatter of the birds. At least none he would father.

The state of disrepair that had fallen upon the house had shocked Zane. The housekeeper he'd hired five months earlier to care for the place had said little of its condition. Upon his arrival three months ago, Zane immediately ordered repairs. It soon became evident that a new furnace and updated electrical system would only scratch the surface of what needed to be done.

That was when he'd decided to call Jordan Larabee, a good friend and a well-known Chicago contractor. Jordan had recommended that Lesley Walker, an architect, have a look at the house and offer a few suggestions. Zane agreed to talk to the woman.

He had to admit that he was going through a lot of trouble and expense for a house he didn't plan to live in long enough to enjoy.

A car turned off the main road and into his driveway. Zane checked his watch. Lesley Walker was punctual—he'd say that for her. The car slowed and pulled to a stop in the circular driveway in front of the house.

The door to the driver's side opened and one long, shapely leg appeared. The body that followed fulfilled the promise of that one leg. The woman was tall, agile and strikingly attractive. She wore a gray business suit: jacket and straight skirt. Zane approved. Her chestnut-colored hair bounced against the top of her shoulders as she turned toward him. Her deep, dark eyes met his and she was unable to hide her shock.

Occasionally Zane forgot about the scar that marked his face. It started at the corner of his left eye and cut a jagged line that crisscrossed down his cheek, ending below his lip. The scar, like the ache in his leg, was a reminder of a debt yet to be collected.

In the past year, he'd discovered how uncomfortable the general public was with infirmities. He shouldn't expect Ms. Walker to react differently than anyone else. In her eyes, like in those of the children in the nearby town, he was a monster.

Zane was mildly surprised when she didn't look away as others routinely did. Instead, she held his gaze. Most people, he'd discovered, were uneasy with less than perfection. Her eyes softened and something passed between them. Something warm. Something gentle. Something strong.

Zane was uncomfortable with softness. He'd known little of it in his formative years, and avoided it by choice as an adult. It was a luxury he could ill afford in his chosen profession. As a soldier of fortune, he had learned early on to freeze out his emotions. Out of necessity, he held back any part of himself that made him vulnerable.

"Ms. Walker?" Zane asked crisply and moved toward the porch stairs.

"Yes, and you must be Zane Ackerman." She stood in the center of the walkway to examine his home. He noticed the way her gaze widened with appreciation as she took in the front of the house. "This is beautiful."

"Thank you. I appreciate you making the drive," he continued, his voice clipped and businesslike.

Her gaze turned back to him, and against his will he was drawn into the warm gentleness that surrounded her. "I enjoyed it." She returned to her vehicle, reached inside her car and brought out a thick writing tablet. "I'll admit Jordan's phone call piqued my interest."

Once again she looked toward the house, and Zane had the opportunity to study her. She was lovely in ways he found difficult to define. If ever he was tempted to get to know a woman, it was now. But Lesley Walker was an emotional luxury he dare not indulge himself with—not while Schuyler lived.

Zane smiled to himself as he watched the appreciation Lesley felt for his home reveal itself in her eyes. With all its flaws, after years of neglect and indifference, she saw the beauty it had once been and would be again. Lesley Walker wasn't superficial—she saw beneath the obvious. Without being aware of what he was doing, his hand went to his face. Only when his fingers touched his scarred cheek did he realize what he'd done. Unnerved by the effect she had on him, he dropped his hand and returned his attention to the architect.

"I'm so pleased Jordan thought to contact me," Lesley said with enthusiasm and walked up to the porch to meet him.

They exchanged brief handshakes and she handed him a business card. Zane noticed she wasn't wearing a wedding band and wondered how it was that a

woman he sensed to be as wholesome and maternal as
Lesley would not be married.

"Would you like to see the inside first?" he asked,
struggling to maintain emotional distance. It would be
far too easy to lower his guard with her, but that was
something Zane couldn't—wouldn't—allow.

"I'd love to see the house."

Zane led the way through the front door. Many of
the rooms were small and he had thought to open them
up. He mentioned his ideas for the remodeling project. Without comment, Lesley wrote down his suggestions, then asked a series of pertinent questions,
taking note of his responses.

"I found the original plans for the house tucked
away in a cabinet in the library."

"If you don't mind, I'd like to take them with me
and read them over," she said, as they walked from
room to room. Every now and again she pointed out
small details he'd barely noticed himself after a few
months of living there.

When they came to the library, he rolled back the
double-wide mahogany doors and waited for her reaction. This was Zane's favorite room. Rooted in his
memory was a picture of his grandfather sitting by the
fireplace, smoking his pipe and reading. It was something he often did himself, sans the pipe. Zane spent
more time in the library than in any of the other
rooms.

"Oh, my," Lesley whispered as though she were
standing on holy ground. "This is perfect just the way
it is—I wouldn't change a thing."

Zane felt that way himself. He wanted nothing al-
tered in this one room, and that she immediately

sensed his feelings boded well for her working on this project.

"Mr. Zane, I was thinking about dinner and—" His housekeeper, Mrs. Applegate, sauntered toward him and stopped abruptly. "Oh, I do apologize. I didn't realize you had company."

"It's no trouble," he answered, quick to reassure her.

His cook was a round, gentle soul who made it her mission in life to spoil him, despite his protests. Nothing he said seemed to discourage her from mothering him. After a while, he gave up trying.

Mrs. Applegate's eyes twinkled with delight when Zane introduced her to Lesley. "It's time Mr. Zane brought a woman into this house."

"Ms. Walker is the architect I mentioned earlier," he said, rankled by the way the elderly woman linked him romantically with Lesley.

"Oh, what a shame." She looked downright disappointed. "Once you finish looking over the house, you let me know," the elderly woman insisted. "I'll set the tea to brewing and bring it to the library. I'm sure you're going to have lots to talk over, and there's no better place to do it than right here with a spot of tea."

Zane might have declined if Lesley hadn't said, "That would be lovely, thank you."

"It's my pleasure." Mrs. Applegate's eyes were filled with devilment as she skirted past Zane. Knowing his housekeeper, there would be far more than tea on that tray. He swore the woman baked enough sweets to keep a dentist in practice. Not a day passed when she didn't set some new confection before him. She seemed to make it her mission in life to put a "little meat on his bones."

"What a sweetheart," Lesley commented, her gaze following the housekeeper.

Zane's reply was unintelligible on purpose. He was grateful to Martha Applegate, but he didn't like the subtle way the woman attempted to work her way into his life. He had a mother, one he preferred to forget, as it happened.

He'd hired Martha Applegate sight unseen a week after he'd decided to take up residence. He needed someone to open up the house and get things in order before he moved to Sleepy Valley.

After viewing the library, Zane led Lesley up the stairs to the six bedrooms situated on the second floor. It was difficult for him to make the trek with his bum leg. Pain shot through his thigh as he climbed. He gritted his teeth, unwilling to show his discomfort.

Once again, Lesley made a series of notations and asked him a number of questions. Standing in the narrow hallway outside the master bedroom, she turned full circle, made a note on the tablet and then glanced his way and smiled.

"How about the kitchen next?"

"Sure." It might have been his imagination, but it seemed that her walk slowed as they descended the staircase. Despite the pain, he increased his step, unwilling to accept allowances for his injuries.

When they entered the kitchen, Mrs. Applegate was nowhere to be seen, which was just as well. Lesley seemed to be filled with enthusiastic ideas. She quickly started to write, her hand moving like a blur over the page. Again she didn't share her thoughts with him.

She happened to look out the kitchen window and then turned to him.

"Those are the stables," he explained.

"And the man?"

"Carl Saks. He lives in the guest house." Carl was a friend and a former mercenary who'd decided to retire in the same area. He'd been looking for property himself. Unable to sit idle, Carl had become a handyman of sorts around the place. Because of his physical limitations, Zane was grateful for the help.

When Lesley finished writing, she pressed the notepad against her breast. "I think that about does it, unless there's something else you'd care to show me." Her eyes landed on the pot of tea Mrs. Applegate had set out, along with a plate heaped high with a fresh batch of chocolate chip cookies.

Over the years, Zane had developed a sixth sense about danger. It had served him well and saved his sorry butt more times than he could count. A half hour with Lesley Walker and he realized this woman was double jeopardy. The best thing he could do for them both was to get her out of his life. And fast.

He made a show of looking at his watch. "I believe you've seen everything necessary. If you're finished, I'll see you to the door."

A look of surprise and affront showed in her expressive face. The friendliness drained from her eyes and she stiffened into a businesslike stance. "Of course. Thank you for your time, Mr. Ackerman."

He escorted her out of the kitchen, stopped in the library long enough to retrieve the blueprints he'd mentioned earlier and then led the way to the front entry.

They exchanged swift handshakes.

"When can I expect to see your ideas?" he asked, and the eagerness with which he posed the question surprised even him.

"I can have them to you next week. Would that be soon enough?"

"Perfect," he answered, the lone word clipped and abrupt.

He stood on the porch and waited until she was inside her car before he turned away. The urge to slam the door was almost more than he could resist. The anger that festered inside him was sharp, raw and completely irrational.

He'd only met Lesley Walker, and if the Fates were with him, the necessity of seeing her again would be minimal. She had yet to pull out of his driveway, and already he was worrying about how long it would be before he could see her again.

This woman was dangerous. Instinctively Zane recognized the threat she represented to his sanity. It was unfortunate. He would have enjoyed getting to know Lesley Walker, but he could see no purpose in developing any kind of relationship when he fully expected to be dead within the year.

Lesley caught her reflection in the rearview mirror and saw that her mouth had formed into a tight line. "That, my dear," she whispered to herself, "was a brush-off." She wondered what she'd said or done to offend the great and mighty Zane Ackerman.

One thing was sure, he was by far the most unusual man she'd ever met. Compelling. Forceful. Handsome. Even with the scar that ran down one side of his face. And the limp seemed to enhance the sense of overwhelming masculinity.

When Jordan Larabee had contacted her about this project, he'd been uncharacteristically closemouthed about the man he was sending her to meet. All Jordan had said was that he'd appreciate it if she'd look over the project and get back to him.

The request was unusual in itself. The fact that it came from Jordan made it more so.

Lesley worked for one of the largest and best-known architectural firms in Chicago. Remodeling projects were not her expertise. Most recently, she'd worked on the plans for a high-rise apartment building. She was responsible for the design of a new city library and the year before, a large government building. Jordan knew all that and yet he'd personally requested she be the one to look at Zane Ackerman's home.

Lesley's relationship with Jordan was finally back on an even keel. They'd once dated while Jordan had been separated from his wife, and had gotten serious enough to discuss the possibility of marriage.

At the time, Lesley had agreed to Jordan's stipulation that there be no children. After the death of his infant son to SIDS, Jordan had refused to consider a family. But, as it turned out, Jordan had reunited with his wife.

It had never set well with Lesley that she was dating a man who remained technically married. When their relationship had progressed to the point that they were serious enough to contemplate making a commitment, Lesley had insisted Jordan go ahead with the divorce. Unfortunately he hadn't a clue where his wife, Molly, was.

Then Jordan discovered that she was working as a nurse in the politically unstable country of Manuka in Africa. And despite Lesley's protests, he had insisted upon going after her himself.

Far more than a rescue had taken place the day Jordan found Molly. Less than three months after the other woman's return to Chicago, Lesley learned that Molly was pregnant. Their daughter was born six months later and within the last year they'd had a son.

Lesley was happy for the couple, and wished them her best. In retrospect, she recognized she hadn't been in love with Jordan Larabee. Instead, she had been in love with the idea of being married. The idea of being a wife. Frankly, it appealed to her now as much as it had three years earlier, but she wasn't as desperate as she'd been the year she turned thirty. If she met the right man, she'd be thrilled. Ecstatic. But frankly, she had given up hope of that happening.

In the time since her breakup with Jordan, she had dated a number of men. But they seemed to fall into two distinct classifications: the disillusioned and the unfit. She wasn't interested in either group.

As she drove down the long driveway that led back to the highway, Lesley realized that because she was interested in the house, she hadn't paid any attention to the view of Lake Michigan. Now the view flashed before her like a shooting star blazing across a velvet night. She literally slammed her foot on the brake.

The car jolted to an abrupt stop. For a moment she did nothing but sit and stare, the view as spectacular as any she'd seen. The blue sky reflected upon the water's white-capped surface like a shiny mirror. Gulls circled overhead and fluffy clouds billowed past.

Hardly aware of what she was doing, Lesley turned off the engine and climbed out of the car. She didn't mean to trespass as she walked across the large expanse of manicured lawn, but she couldn't help herself.

She'd wandered some distance when she stumbled upon a viewpoint. A stone bench was situated at the

edge of the drop-off. Clusters of blooming red roses
scented the afternoon air.

After standing and admiring the view for several
moments, Lesley sat down and breathed in the calm
beauty of the scene before her. There was water for as
far as the eye could see. Sailboats with their bright
spinnakers dotted the surface. Motorboats zoomed
past, their wakes rippling wider and wider swells.

For no reason Lesley could understand, she battled
back tears. It was as though this house, this property... this man lured her very soul.

She'd sensed it the moment she'd turned into the
driveway. Felt it to the very marrow of her bones. The
house had called out to her like a wailing spirit. A
small voice buried deep inside her heart had welcomed her home. Because she was practical, she'd refused to believe, refused to listen.

That was when she first noticed Zane standing on
the porch, waiting for her arrival. One look at the
forceful, enigmatic man and she had felt as though all
the oxygen had emptied from her lungs. Never had she
reacted to a man quite this way.

Even now she was left to wonder what had happened between them those first few moments. Neither chose to voice whatever it was, and both seemed
equally uncomfortable with the force of the attraction.

Later, Zane couldn't seem to get rid of her fast
enough, and Lesley was convinced that whatever had
transpired had all been one-sided.

Now she wasn't so sure.

A sound behind her alerted her to the fact that she
was no longer alone. Lesley stood and turned to face

the man who'd dominated her thoughts from the moment they'd met.

Zane sat atop a black gelding, his dark gaze focused on her. "I thought you'd left."

Embarrassed to have been found trespassing, Lesley cleared her throat and licked her lips before she forced herself to smile. "Hello again," she greeted. Zane made an intimidating figure sitting atop the sleek Arabian, staring down on her. Because the sun was behind him, it made it all the more difficult to read his expression, but she couldn't help feeling that he was displeased to find her still on his property. "I hope you don't mind that I stopped to admire the view."

The temperamental gelding jerked his head, and shifted his two hind legs in an impatient two-step. With a flick of the reins, Zane quieted the imposing beast.

"It's so beautiful here," Lesley added, hoping that was explanation enough. She glanced at her watch, startled by how much time had passed. It seemed she'd only been a matter of minutes, but she'd been sitting there nearly an hour.

She should say something, anything, but it was as if his happening upon her like this had frozen her thought processes. She knew that had she tried to explain, she would have made an even greater fool of herself, which was something she wasn't eager to do. She didn't know what Zane must think of her.

"This was my grandmother's favorite spot," Zane surprised her by saying. He didn't sound displeased with her. If anything, she heard puzzlement in his voice, as if she were the last person he expected to find on his property.

"Your grandmother?" she repeated, not realizing that there was a family connection with the house.

"The house belonged to my grandparents," he admitted gruffly, as though he resented her knowing even this small bit of information. The Arabian's impatient jig continued. "How much longer do you intend to stay?"

"I really must get back to the office. I should have left right away. I really am sorry if I did something I shouldn't have." She backed away from him.

"It's fine, Lesley," he said so softly, she wasn't sure Zane was the one who'd spoken or if it was that small voice she'd heard earlier. The voice in her own heart. The one that had welcomed her with open arms.

Lesley didn't sleep that night. Every time she closed her eyes, it was Zane Ackerman's face that came into view. He'd been both rude and unfriendly, and yet she was physically drawn to him with a force so powerful, it left her senses reeling even now.

The next morning the first thing Lesley did when she reached the office was put a call through to Jordan Larabee.

"How do you know Zane Ackerman?" she asked without so much as greeting him.

"Good morning to you, too," Jordan said, his amusement echoing over the line. "I take it you drove out to meet Zane yesterday."

"Yes."

"How is he, by the way?"

"Fine. I take it he's a friend of yours."

"We go way back."

"Tell me about him." After a sleepless night, Lesley wasn't up to playing cat-and-mouse games with Jordan.

"What do you want to know?"

"Is he married?" That this would be the first question she put before him shocked even her. Although the question had been paramount in her mind, she never intended to blurt it out. She hoped to ease into it with far more subtlety.

To her dismay, Jordan laughed outright. "So that's the way the ball bounces?"

"What do you mean by that?" She sounded defensive, and that irritated her all the more.

"You're irresistibly drawn to his bad-boy image. Well, Lesley, I hate to say it, but you aren't alone. I've never met a woman who wasn't intrigued by Zane Ackerman. I don't know what it is about him, but whatever it is, he's got it in spades."

"I'm not interested in him that way," she said with far less conviction than she felt.

"And pigs fly."

"He was rude and he couldn't seem to get me out of his house fast enough."

"That's Zane all right."

Her comments seemed to amuse Jordan all the more.

"What happened to him? The injuries look recent."

"He never said," Jordan answered, "and I never asked."

Lesley bit her lower lip. "I fell in love with the house. I'm working on another project now, but I'll look over my notes and get back to you by the end of the week."

"Perfect," Jordan responded, but he sounded distracted. Like her, Jordan was a busy man. Neither one of them had the time to chitchat. "Let me know if you need anything."

"I will," she promised.

"Thanks, Les," Jordan said affectionately. "I appreciate you doing this, and I know Zane does, too."

"I'm glad to help." As she replaced the telephone receiver, Lesley wondered if she'd feel the same way later. She had the distinct impression that this assignment wasn't going to be like her normal projects.

Zane wandered down to the breakfast table early the following morning. Mrs. Applegate was humming cheerfully to herself as she stood in front of the stove.

"Such a nice young woman," she said, smiling over at Zane as she poured him a cup of coffee.

"Who?" he asked, pretending not to know.

"That architect who stopped by yesterday afternoon."

Zane didn't respond one way or another. An achy, restless feeling had come over him the moment Lesley Walker had driven away. The sensation had stayed with him all night. Generally, the pain in his leg was what kept him awake. Not thoughts of a woman. Especially one he barely knew. One thing was certain, he had no intention of furthering the relationship.

The back door opened and Carl stepped inside the kitchen. "Morning," he grumbled with a decided lack of friendliness. He walked over to where Zane sat and pulled out a chair. "I've been thinking of changing feed stores," his friend announced starkly. Carl had taken over ordering the supplies and other duties to keep himself from going stir-crazy.

"I thought we got a good price at Hoffman Feed."

Mrs. Applegate delivered plates heaped with crisp fried bacon, eggs and toast to the two men.

"The prices are fine," Carl answered before digging into his breakfast. He ate like a man who feared this would be his last meal.

Zane knew his friend well enough to realize something was troubling him, and he suspected it had little to do with the local feed store. To the best of his knowledge, Carl had been buying whatever he needed from the same place since the horses had been delivered. Their prices were fair and Zane preferred to do business locally. But if Carl wanted to drive another twenty miles to another feed store, Zane figured that was his business.

"You got a problem with Hoffman Feed?"

Carl paused, the fork poised in front of his mouth while he analyzed the question. "I don't much care for sassy women."

Zane lowered his head in an effort to hide his amusement. So Carl had clashed swords with Candy Hoffman again. It wasn't the first time the two had created sparks.

"I saw a woman wandering around the grounds yesterday. Who was she?" Carl asked.

"The architect," Zane answered without elaborating.

"A real sweetheart, too, if you ask me," Mrs. Applegate called from the other side of the kitchen.

Zane hadn't asked, but he knew if he mentioned it his housekeeper would ignore him, and so he said nothing.

"She was a pretty thing," Carl said. "Will she be visiting again anytime soon?"

"I don't know." Zane eyed his fellow mercenary, disliking the interest Carl revealed in Lesley.

"If she does, how about an introduction?"

Zane didn't like the idea one bit, but before he could say so, Mrs. Applegate approached the table and set down a plate of hot-from-the-oven cinnamon rolls. "She isn't the one for you."

"Who isn't?" Carl barked the question as he reached for a roll, burning his fingers in the process. He licked his fingertips and cursed under his breath.

"Candy Hoffman has her eye on you," the housekeeper informed him.

Carl didn't bother hiding his irritation. "That woman's meaner than a beaver with a broomstick up her butt."

Mrs. Applegate chuckled, and shook her head. "That's not the way I see it. It seems to me you're just as sweet on her, only you don't like it. Come to think of it, Candy isn't all that pleased about it neither."

Carl snorted loudly. "I'd rather be skinned alive than have anything more to do with that woman. She's unreasonable, irrational, pigheaded, and that's just for starters. If I never see her again, it'd suit me just fine." Having said that much, the former mercenary leapt up from the chair and headed out the door. He turned back abruptly and reached for the cinnamon roll. "I'll be buying the feed elsewhere," he said in a way that challenged Zane to defy him.

"Get it wherever you want," Zane told him.

Carl cast a triumphant look toward the housekeeper and headed out the back door. To his surprise, Mrs. Applegate burst out laughing. "Life's too short for green bananas."

Baffled, Zane studied the older woman. She had a habit of saying the most nonsensical things, and then looking for him to agree with her.

Zane raised both hands. "I'm staying out of this," he announced.

The housekeeper didn't seem to mind.

One thing she'd said did make sense. Life was too short, and for him, it was getting shorter every day.

Chapter Two

"I say he's likely a gangster."

The words struck Lesley as odd, and captured her attention. She'd stopped to fill up her car with gas in Sleepy Valley, the community closest to Zane's home.

The gas station attendant filling the vehicle in the space next to hers slowly shook his head. "Just because he's up there in that huge house all alone doesn't make him a hit man."

"It ain't normal, living up there the way he does." The middle-aged man in the car wasn't so easily swayed. "Makes me wonder if anyone asked the right questions before letting him move into our community. We've got a responsibility to the good people in this town."

"He isn't alone," the attendant filling Lesley's car contradicted. "Martha Applegate is keeping his house, and from what Candy Hoffman said, there's another man there, as well."

"Yeah, but it isn't anyone we know."

The other station attendant scratched the side of his head. "I can't say that I've talked to him, but he minds his own business, doesn't he?"

"Yes, but exactly what type of business is he minding?" the man inside the car asked. "That's what worries me."

The three men exchanged knowing looks.

"When was the last time he came into town?"

"I haven't got a clue. Personally I've only seen him the one time."

"That's what I thought. He mostly keeps to himself. It ain't natural—that's all I'm saying."

The attendant who was washing Lesley's window paused in the middle of his task. "My guess is he's involved in drugs."

"Drugs," the customer repeated as if this were a new thought.

Lesley managed to smother a giggle. She could well imagine what Zane would say if he were listening in on this conversation himself. He'd be as amused as she was. Amused or outraged.

"Some people say he's a monster," Lesley said, unable to keep quiet any longer.

The man in the space opposite hers turned and stared at her. "It makes one wonder what happened to his face, doesn't it?"

"I can't understand why he doesn't have reconstructive surgery," the first attendant stated. "Seems to me that someone who could afford to live in that house wouldn't be hurting for money."

"Maybe he likes the idea of frightening children," the other attendant suggested.

"Children, nothing. He makes my blood run cold every time I see him." The customer closed his eyes and cringed.

Lesley paid for her gas. It was difficult to keep a straight face, but she managed. And people thought women gossiped!

By the time she arrived at Zane's house, Lesley's amusement had turned to resentment. It irritated her that people could be so cruel. Zane was no more a drug lord than she was, and as for him keeping to himself . . . well, everyone was entitled to privacy.

She rang the doorbell and waited. Mrs. Applegate opened the front door. The moment she saw Lesley, the housekeeper's face brightened with a warm smile.

"It's so good to see you again, dearie. Mr. Zane's out, but he'll be back any minute. You make yourself comfortable in the library and I'll bring you a spot of tea." She led the way into the room that Lesley had loved best.

"I'm sure Mr. Zane will be along shortly."

"It's no problem, Mrs. Applegate. I'm early." Lesley had given herself plenty of time to make the drive in from the heart of downtown Chicago. Being that it was Friday, she had fully anticipated running into heavy weekend traffic.

But her eagerness had a lot more to do with seeing Zane again than with any traffic problems. Far more. She needed to see him. Needed to test this strange attraction. The fact of the matter was that she'd left the office far earlier than necessary, and very little of her reason had to do with the renovation project.

In the past week, Lesley had devoted hour upon hour to this project, far and above what time she'd originally allotted. She studied the original blueprints, blending her ideas for the renovation in with the original work, modernizing the house so that the new merged naturally with old. Her goal was that anyone who stepped into the house for the first time would never guess that part of the home had been changed.

True to her word, Mrs. Applegate returned a few moments later with a cup of tea and a thick slice of chocolate cake. She chatted briefly then quietly slipped away.

Carrying the teacup with her, Lesley walked over to the bookcase and read the titles. Many of the books were ones she'd read and enjoyed herself. More than any other room of the house, she sensed Zane's personality strongest here. The furniture was leather, new and stiff. There were no pictures, no artwork—just the leather sofa, two chairs and more books than in some libraries.

When Lesley least expected it, the mahogany doors glided open and Zane entered the room, closing the panels behind him. She turned, certain that she'd embellished his impact on her in the days since their meeting. If anything, she found him even more compelling than she had the first time. He was a hard man—whether from necessity or nature, she couldn't be sure. Intuitively she recognized he was an honorable one, as well.

His eyes revealed none of his feelings, but she sensed that he was pleased to see her again, the same way she felt toward him. No one needed to tell her that Zane didn't want to feel anything for her. But he did, and she gained a good deal of pleasure in the knowledge.

"Hello, Lesley."

"Zane." She sounded slightly breathless; indeed, that was the way she felt.

"You brought the blueprints?"

It didn't escape her notice how eager he was to get down to business. The sooner she was in and out of his house and his life, the better. He all but painted a banner to tell her as much.

"I have several things to show you."

"I'm anxious to start on the remodeling," he said matter-of-factly.

A polite knock sounded against the library door.

"Yes," Zane called out.

Mrs. Applegate slid open the door. "I'm sorry to disturb you but Candy Hoffman is here to see you."

Lesley watched as Zane frowned. A woman. Lesley's stomach clenched with what she could only determine to be an unflattering form of jealousy. It was crazy to feel any such thing, especially over a woman she had never met.

"I'm sure this won't take long," Zane offered apologetically to Lesley.

"Can I show her in?" Mrs. Applegate asked.

Zane nodded, but Lesley could see he was none-too-pleased with the interruption.

A lanky blonde walked into the room, and looked around nervously. She wore faded jeans, a checkered shirt and cowboy boots. Her short hairstyle didn't complement her looks. Lesley guessed the other woman to be in her late twenties, perhaps early thirties, close to her own age.

"I'm sorry to disturb you, Mr. Ackerman," the other woman said nervously. Her blue eyes appeared apologetic. "I learned this morning that you've decided to buy your supplies elsewhere."

"That's right."

"I was wondering if there's been a problem with the goods or service Hoffman Feed has given you?"

"On the contrary," Zane said matter-of-factly. "As far as I can tell, both have been excellent."

Candy opened her mouth as if to argue, then promptly snapped it shut with a look of surprise. "Then, if you don't mind my asking, what made you decide to give your business to another feed store?"

Zane didn't hesitate. "I can't rightly say. Carl makes those kind of decisions. He asked me about it recently and I told him the decision was his."

"Carl Saks?" Her eyes rounded with what Lesley would best describe as distress. She lowered her head. "I was afraid of that."

"Afraid?"

Candy nodded. "Carl and I seem to have a personality conflict."

"Carl isn't unreasonable," Zane offered. "Perhaps you should talk to him."

Candy shook her head adamantly. "I'd rather peel grapes than deal with that man. He's stubborn and irrational."

A hint of a smile eased up the good side of Zane's mouth. "As I recall, Carl said much the same thing about you."

Candy's head shot up, and her eyes flashed with outrage. "Maybe I will talk with him after all. All I'm asking, Mr. Ackerman, is that you don't make a rash decision about not giving us your business. You have a big account with us and we don't want to lose it."

"I hope you can work things out with Carl, then," Zane said.

"I'll do my best," she muttered as she spun around and headed out the door.

As soon as the other woman was out of sight, Zane chuckled softly.

Lesley wasn't sure what was happening, but she had a pretty good guess. Zane turned back to face her and smiled. "You know, I almost feel sorry for Carl. It looks to me that at long last he's met his match."

Carl wasn't the only one, Lesley mused. If she had anything to say about it, Zane Ackerman had found his equal in her, as well.

Candy Hoffman hadn't a clue what she was going to say to Carl. She never had been fond of crow, and knowing the man, he'd make sure she downed it, feathers and all. Candy wasn't sure what had gone wrong, but the two of them had started off on the wrong foot and it had gone steadily downhill from there. The last straw had come when he stopped off at the feed store a few days ago, asking about his order. Candy had seen to it herself only that morning and sent it out. Or so she thought. When Carl insisted it hadn't been delivered, she swore it had been. Later she found the order in the back. She'd sent it out right away, but apparently that wasn't good enough.

As she expected, she found Carl working in the barn, mucking stalls. Great. Just great. He was bound to be in an ugly mood.

"Hello, Carl," she said, tucking her fingertips in her back jean pockets.

He glanced over his shoulder, saw it was her and continued shoveling.

Candy swallowed tightly. She'd be tarred and feathered before she'd grovel to this man, but there might be a way around that.

"It seems you and I got started on the wrong foot," she said, hoping that would suffice.

Carl said nothing.

"I'm here to mend fences. I regret the argument we had the other day about your order. I was at fault, and I apologize."

Again he pretended not to hear her.

"What is it you want from me?" she asked, losing her limited patience.

"You're here because you don't want to lose this account."

"All right," she shouted, kicking the toe of her cowboy boot against the floorboards. "I don't want to lose this account."

"Let me ask you something." He turned around and glared at her.

"All right." She was eager to do what she could to right the wrongs committed.

"Are you a man or a woman?"

The anger that burned inside her was fierce, but she managed to hold on to it. "I don't understand the question."

Carl leaned against the shovel handle. "When I first met you, I thought you were a man. It wasn't until you spoke that I realized you were a woman."

Candy bristled. "What's that got to do with anything?"

"Your legs aren't bad, either."

From another man, Candy might have found the words complimentary, but not from Carl. "My being male or female has nothing to do with the feed store. We give you good service and excellent prices."

"I don't like your attitude." Carl slapped the shovel against the side of the stall and advanced toward her.

Candy didn't budge an inch. She refused to allow him to intimidate her.

"You've got a temper."

"Me!" she protested.

"You're bossy as hell."

"I most certainly am not!" She couldn't believe what she was hearing. True, she'd crossed swords with Carl every time he was in the store, but that wasn't her fault. At least not entirely.

"The fact is, I don't like you."

"The fact is, I don't think much of you, either. You can forget I came by.... It was an obvious mistake. Take your business elsewhere." She spun around, eager now to make her escape. Pride was the only thing that prevented her from running out of the barn.

She hadn't gone more than a couple of steps, when Carl reached out and grabbed her by the upper arm. Against her will, she came whirling back around with such force that she collided against his chest.

Carl seemed as surprised as she was herself, and now that he'd trapped her, he didn't seem to know what to do with her. Fierce pride filled his eyes until they glittered with bronze fire. He drew her more firmly up against him and then lowered his mouth to hers.

Candy was too shocked to react, too stunned to respond. She meant to protest. No man in all her life had ever made her more angry. No man had defied her the way Carl Saks had. No man had stood up against her the way he had, either.

Against every dictate of her will, she parted her lips. His tongue plunged forward into the small opening, dominating her, taming her, seducing her.

Squirming, she protested, but he plowed his free hand into her hair and held her head prisoner while he dominated her in the most primitive of ways.

It didn't take Candy long to realize she was waging a losing battle. She didn't want this, and at the same moment, she was working her mouth against his, giving as well as receiving.

Before she was aware of what was happening, the intensity of the kiss changed. All the fight seemed to go out of them both at precisely the same moment. He started to withdraw his tongue when she met his with soft, gentle touches of her own.

Carl groaned and Candy melted against him.

The kiss went on and on until Candy wasn't sure she ever wanted it to end. Carl was the one who came to his senses first. He eased his mouth from hers, dropped his arms and stepped back.

Candy raised the back of her hand to her mouth and pressed it there, all the while staring at him. Tears blurred her eyes. Tears of anger. Tears of outrage and denial.

Earlier pride had dictated that she not run from him. He'd stripped her of that. He'd claimed far more than a kiss. He'd robbed her of her dignity. With a sob choking her throat, she reeled around and raced out of the barn as fast as her legs would carry her.

She thought she heard Carl call her name, but she didn't stop running until she reached the truck. Never, she silently vowed, would she ever return.

* * *

"I like what you've done," Zane told Lesley. *Liked* was an understatement. Her ideas for the renovation were incredible. Better than he dared hope. That she'd spent an incredible amount of time and effort on the project was evident on every page.

"I gave Jordan a copy and he said he'd look over the plans and give you an estimate the first part of next week."

Zane's original intention had been to be as quick with this meeting as humanly possible. He'd look over the drawings simply to be polite and then explain that he had a pressing appointment and send Lesley back to the city. When he was alone, he'd review the drawings again.

The minute Lesley had shown him her ideas, Zane was enthralled. She had captured the very soul of this home, taken the best of what he loved about the place and made it better. Some of the changes were dramatic. Walls removed. Rooms created. Others changes were subtle.

Zane pored over the prints, and each time he studied them he saw something more. He should be alarmed, he told himself. This woman, who knew little more about him than his given name, had captured the very essence of who he was. With that knowledge, she'd created for him a home any man would treasure. A home meant for a family. The family his vengeance would cost him.

Zane had insulated his life and yet, Lesley, after one brief encounter, had seen through the protective barrier he'd placed around his heart as if it were as clear as cellophane.

Alarm bells buzzed, but he ignored them.

"I have a decorator friend I'd like to recommend," Lesley was saying.

They were both leaning against the table. Zane turned to listen and realized something. He wanted to make love to Lesley. He didn't want her to matter to him. Couldn't afford the extravagance of falling in love. Especially not now. Not ever, if he was going to follow through with his plans. But the need to hold her, to feel her mouth under his, was nearly overwhelming.

He didn't want to care about her, and in that same instant realized he was too late. He already did care.

A knock sounded behind him and Mrs. Applegate let herself into the library. "Dinner's ready," she announced with a smile so big, it looked as if she'd tried to eat a banana sideways. "I took the liberty of setting a place for Lesley," she said.

"It's dinnertime?" Zane didn't realize how late it was.

"I must be going."

"Please stay for dinner." He wasn't sure what he felt. It went without saying that he would like for her to stay, but he also knew that the less time they spent together, the better.

"I should be getting back to the city," Lesley murmured, rolling the prints back up.

"Nonsense," Zane found himself telling her.

She hesitated. "You're sure?"

"Positive." He was equally confident that he was about to make the biggest mistake of his life, but even that didn't seem to be enough to keep him from leaping off the edge of the cliff.

Mrs. Applegate had set the dining room table, and Zane nearly groaned aloud when he saw there were only two place settings.

"Carl is having dinner in town tonight," his housekeeper informed him even before he could voice the question.

That was just hunky-dory.

"I'm sure you'd like to freshen up before dinner," Martha was saying to Lesley.

The two women disappeared. Zane walked over to the window and looked out. It usually didn't get dark until after eight this time of year. But it was just after six and already the sky was black.

He looked toward the water and realized that a storm was brewing. Angry, forbidding clouds threatened the sky and the wind was picking up.

Zane thought to warn Lesley and suggest that she start for the city now, then thought better of it. He'd worry if the storm broke and she was on the road. It was best to ride it out and send her off when the worst of it had passed.

Lesley returned a few minutes later and they sat opposite each other at the dining room table. Mrs. Applegate had outdone herself. There was roast chicken, mashed potatoes and country gravy, fresh green beans and biscuits. Zane swore his housekeeper's buttermilk biscuits melted in his mouth.

When they'd finished, Martha brought in two cups of coffee. "In the words of Shirley MacLaine," Lesley told him, "that was the best meal I've had in three thousand years."

Zane laughed loudly, enjoying her joke. He stopped when he realized she was staring. He didn't laugh often and forgot about the scar that twisted his face and what his amusement must look like to her.

"Don't stop," she pleaded. "It's just that was the first time I'd ever heard you laugh out loud. You should do it more often."

Lesley smiled at him—a soft, intimate smile. The kind a woman gives a man she loves. Being with her made him feel happy deep inside. He'd sensed that danger earlier, and chose to ignore it. This architect made him weak in ways he had yet to understand.

The discordant sound of thunder crashing outside fell like a hammer against an anvil into the center of the room.

Lesley gasped at the unexpectedness of it.

The lights blinked. There'd been a number of storms in the few months following his arrival. Such a storm as this was what had convinced Zane to have the house rewired.

Lesley stood and walked over to the window. She edged forward and examined the angry sky Zane had viewed thirty minutes earlier.

He'd forgotten to mention the incoming squall over dinner, and wanted to kick himself. The omission hadn't been intentional; he'd gotten caught up in their conversation and the matter had slipped his mind.

The lights went out with the second peal of thunder. Luckily it was light enough inside the house to locate the candles.

Lesley helped clear the table.

When the rain started it pounded like angry fists against the windows. "I better check the horses," Zane said. Since Carl was away for the evening, someone would need to quiet them.

"You go with him," he heard Mrs. Applegate insist. Rather than argue with them both, Zane let her.

He started out the back door. Lesley found a sweater on a hook just inside the porch. She held it over her head as they hurried toward the barn.

The horses whinnied and stomped their front legs when he stepped inside the barn door. It was darker in there.

"Carl?" Zane called, thinking his friend might have returned, but there was no response. He lit a couple of lanterns that he kept for just such emergencies.

The animals needed quieting and Zane did so with the skill of one who is more comfortable with equines than with people. To her credit, Lesley stayed out of his way and let him do what needed to be done. She didn't offer to help, since she was a stranger, and right now his stock needed reassurances from someone they were familiar with.

When he'd finished tying the horses down for the night, refreshing their water and giving them an extra scoop of oats, Zane turned and found Lesley studying him.

She gave him a slow, sweet smile. Earlier, Zane had realized how badly he wanted to make love to her. In that moment, the need increased tenfold. His chest lifted with a deep, sharp intake of breath.

"We better get back to the house," he said, fearing if they stayed in the barn any longer, he wouldn't be able to resist her.

By the time they extinguished the light, it was pitch-black. Zane opened the door and watched as the rain pelted the ground as if it were a means of punishment.

"Maybe we should stay in here for a while," Lesley suggested, staring into the pulsating rain. It was coming down in sheets now.

"I don't think that's such a good idea," Zane said quickly, fearing the level of intimacy would increase beyond his ability to resist her. At the moment he would have welcomed the entire community of Sleepy Valley into his home if it would help him take his mind off touching Lesley.

The temptation grew stronger each passing minute, and their being alone together didn't bode well. Already he could feel his level of resistance weakening.

"You think we should make a run for the house?" She sounded uncertain.

"No," he said, groaning inwardly. To do so would be foolish. Lesley would get drenched in a matter of seconds. The thought of her undressing and him finding warm, dry clothes for her to wear—his clothes—created an equally disturbing picture.

"Zane."

Just the way she said his name told him what she wanted. It was the same thought that had been hounding him from the moment they'd sat down for dinner. He needed her touch. Needed her in his arms. This kind of longing didn't respond to logic.

They reached for each other, clumsy in their efforts to hold one another. The instant her lips slid over his, a hot excitement filled Zane. Instantly he was so hard, he ached. He'd been a long time without a woman, but not that long. Not long enough to warrant this kind of arousal. It felt as if his body were on fire. Empty. Aching. Wanting.

Lesley would never know the level of self-control it demanded not to bury himself hip-deep inside of her right then and there. It wouldn't have taken much to back her against a wall and make love to her.

Something was wrong. Something was very wrong for him to have allowed his control to slip this much. To cause this ache. This physical frustration would only grow worse. He had to put an end to it now, otherwise the consequences would be more than he could afford to pay.

He ground his lips over hers, wanting to punish her for making him want her this badly. Even that tactic didn't work. Her mouth softened, opening under the force of his kiss. When he invaded her lips with his tongue, she gave a small, welcoming cry. Their tongues dueled and mated.

By the time he broke off the kiss, the rush of blood to his head—and other body parts—made him feel as if he were about to explode.

Lesley braced her forehead against his shoulder; her breathing was uneven, and as heavy as his own. Neither spoke, and Zane suspected that they weren't quite sure what there was to say. He'd never meant for any of this to happen, but it had, and God help them both, he didn't have a single regret.

He kissed her again, gently this time. Her mouth met his, her lips warm, wet and pliable. His body reacted instinctively to her, hardening. She started to move against him, her hips making small, nervous rotations against the bulge in his pants. He braced his hands on the wall on each side of her, uncertain that he could withstand the pleasure and not embarrass them both.

She stilled immediately and Zane guessed that she hadn't realized what she was doing.

A noise at the other side of the barn told him they were no longer alone. He broke away from Lesley, and when she stumbled forward, he caught her by the shoulders.

"Who's there?" he barked, resenting the intrusion.

"Carl."

"Where the hell have you been?" he called into the darkness.

"Town." They remained on opposite sides of the barn, and neither one seemed pleased to happen upon the other.

"Who's with you?" The question came from Carl.

"Lesley Walker."

"Who?"

Zane heard Lesley's light laugh.

"Lesley Walker," she called out herself. "The architect."

"Is everything all right with the horses?"

"Yes," Zane snapped, wishing his friend would get the hell out of there.

"All right, all right," Carl muttered. Zane heard the door open and close and heaved a sigh of relief. He'd been angry and impatient with Carl when he should be grateful his friend had intervened when he had. He didn't know how much longer he would have been able to hold on to his control. He'd sensed from the first that Lesley had the power to make him weak, but he hadn't realized just how compelling she was.

"Let's get inside the house," he said, taking her by the hand. Guided by the candle Mrs. Applegate had left burning in the kitchen window, they raced into the night. The distance wasn't great, but by the time they reached the back steps, Zane's thigh felt as if it were on fire. He made it up three steps before his leg gave out on him.

"Zane," Lesley cried, coming back for him.

"I'm all right," he snapped, not wanting her help. With difficulty, he righted himself, using the railing for leverage.

Lesley stood in the pounding rain, ready to assist him should he need her. He bit back the words to tell her to stay away from him and would have uttered them had he found the strength.

Blinded by pain, he stumbled onto the back porch. Moisture fell in droplets down his neck. The water ran like cold fingers down his back.

He made it to the kitchen and into a chair before he collapsed, his shoulders heaving with the effort. Lesley was there in an instant with a towel. That she would be witness to this weakness deeply upset him.

The kitchen door swung open and the housekeeper stepped inside. "You're back," she said cheerfully. "I was beginning to wonder what was taking so long." It was then that she noticed Lesley was soaked to the skin. "Oh, dear, look at you two. You'll catch your death of cold."

"I'm fine," Lesley insisted.

"I insist you get out of those wet things this instant," his housekeeper continued. "Mr. Zane must have something that will fit you, dear. And don't you dare think about driving back to the city on a night like this. I'll have a bed made up for you in a jiffy. We absolutely insist that you spend the night. Isn't that right, Mr. Zane?"

He glared at the older woman and noticed that her mouth was wreathed in the biggest smile he'd ever seen. This was exactly what she wanted. Exactly what she'd planned from the first.

Chapter Three

Lesley woke with a start, and sat up in bed. Her heart pounded solidly against her chest as she surveyed her surroundings. She remembered immediately that she was in Zane's home, and that Mrs. Applegate had insisted she spend the night because of the storm. Lesley hadn't needed a crystal ball to realize that Zane wasn't nearly as eager as his housekeeper for her company.

Lying back, her head nestled against the feather pillow, Lesley reviewed the events of the evening. Zane had approved of her remodeling ideas. They'd pored over the plans for two hours without either one of them aware of the time. Zane had asked her to stay for dinner and then the storm had struck with a vengeance. Because of the thunder and lightning, they'd gone out to the barn to quiet the horses. That was when Zane had kissed her.

Lesley closed her eyes at the memory, longing to recapture the incredible sensation his kisses had aroused. She doubted that she would ever fully understand her immediate and intimate response to this man. Logically, she reminded herself she knew little more than the bare facts about Zane. He knew nothing more of her, either. They were strangers, fighting an attraction as powerful as the strongest magnets. It seemed that a force greater than either one of them was pulling them toward each other. For what purpose, Lesley could only speculate.

A glance at the illuminated dial of her wristwatch told her it was ten minutes after three. It would be hours yet before anyone was up and about. Yet, Lesley doubted she would be able to sleep any longer.

She slipped out of bed, and as quietly as possible opened her bedroom door. Briefly she wondered if the electricity had come back on. The question was answered for her. The soft glow of a gentle light showed below, coming from the library.

Lesley donned the housecoat Mrs. Applegate had left for her. It nearly went around her twice. Looping the sash closed, she padded barefoot down the stairs.

Standing in the library doorway, Lesley realized the dancing flames of the fire provided what light was available. Flickering shadows danced against the walls. A moan captured her attention before she noticed Zane. He sat in the chair with his head tossed back. He gritted his teeth as he rubbed his hand down his injured thigh.

Had she given any thought to what she should do, Lesley realized later, it would have been exactly the opposite of what she did, which was to rush to his side.

"Zane." She knelt on the floor, next to him. "What's wrong? Can I get you anything?"

He opened his eyes and seemed startled to find her there. "No. Just go away." He ground out the order between clenched teeth.

"No," she returned just as adamantly. "Tell me what to do to help you." She felt nearly frantic, unable to bear seeing him in this amount of pain. Earlier in the kitchen, she realized that his leg was hurting him, but it was nothing like this.

"Nothing. You can do nothing," he insisted coldly. He glared at her, silently willing her to leave him, but Lesley refused to budge.

She watched the muscle of his thigh spasm, and because she felt helpless and utterly useless, she placed her hand over his. Her relief was great when he didn't push it aside. Together they worked, vigorously kneading the knotted flesh, working out the cramp. Gradually she could feel the muscle relax.

Breathing heavily, Zane went lax. He dropped his arms and she continued to gently massage the muscle. When she happened to glance up, she noticed he was studying her. His gaze, which had been cutting and angry seconds earlier, was tender now.

"I woke you?" he asked, his voice little more than a whisper. The spasm seemed to have drained him of all strength.

She shook her head. "I don't know what woke me. I thought the lights had come back on."

"Not yet."

"I came down to read. I didn't realize you were here."

Zane's hand briefly cupped her cheek, his touch light and tender. "I didn't mean to snap at you."

She leaned back on her haunches. "Don't apologize. I understand."

"My leg does that sometimes, without rhyme or reason, but the spasms don't generally last this long."

She remembered their dash from the barn to the house and realized the physical exertion had probably contributed to this seizure. "I'm sorry," she whispered, thinking she was probably responsible for this. He would never have felt the need to run for cover if it hadn't been for her.

"You're sorry for my leg?"

She nodded and explained her reasoning. "You haven't been to bed yet. Has your leg ached all evening?"

"No." His intense look held hers for a moment before he sipped from a glass of amber liquid. "I didn't trust myself to go upstairs."

Lesley didn't understand. "Trust yourself?"

A smile that wasn't one of amusement edged up the good side of his mouth. "You tempt me, Lesley, almost more than I can resist."

The low, seductive lilt to his voice made his words the most incredibly beautiful ones Lesley had ever heard.

"I don't know what would have happened if Carl hadn't come into the barn when he did."

"I know," she whispered. "I don't generally... I mean—"

He stopped her before she completed the thought. His voice was hoarse and low. "I realize that."

Lesley didn't know who moved first. It was like it had been earlier, both needing each other, both throwing off their restraints and giving in to the impulse. Only, the impulse was fast becoming a compulsion.

His mouth found hers, his lips warm and moist. He tasted of fine brandy and tenderness. It seemed they were barely able to get enough of each other. Her need was as greedy and demanding as his. Her nipples peaked hard against the thin fabric of the housecoat. He slipped his hand inside the opening and cupped her breast. Lesley tensed as a small moan of satisfaction moved up her throat. His thumb stroked her already-extended nipple. Shivers shot down her spine as she leaned into him. She felt warm and wonderful. Loved and needed.

"I was afraid something like this would happen," he whispered against her ear. His warm breath stirred her hair. Her knees ached from kneeling on the carpet, but she didn't want to move. Their position was awkward for him, too, but neither of them was willing to move.

"Is it true?"

"What?" he whispered as his thumb continued to work its magic with her breast. Soon he had the front of the robe spread open and filled the palms of his hands with her bounty through the thin top.

"You said I tempt you."

He moaned softly and kissed her with a wild kind of hunger, his tongue delving into her mouth, stroking her own, bringing their lovemaking to a near-fever pitch.

When Zane abruptly ended the kiss, Lesley moaned in protest. He stood and led her to the sofa. "I want to see you," he whispered huskily as he undid the sash completely and peeled open the robe. Mrs. Applegate's pajama top was several sizes too large, affording him ample room to slide his hand inside the neckline, but that no longer suited him. One by one, he unfastened the buttons.

"Zane," Lesley whispered, fearing she was about to disappoint him. "I'm not well endowed. I mean . . ."

"Shh," he whispered, and bent forward to gently capture her nipple between his teeth. An electrical jolt of sensation shot through her. His lips fastened more fully upon her breast, and he sucked strongly until she was nearly lifted off the sofa.

Lesley closed her eyes and bit her lower lip. The pleasure was almost more than she could stand. The emptiness inside her began to ache. The desire she felt was physical as well as mental. All these months, all these years she'd been telling herself that she was perfectly content without a man in her life. She had her career, and wonderful friends. She found satisfaction in her outside interests.

Within the space of one evening Zane had proved beyond a shadow of a doubt that she'd been kidding herself. The longing for a husband and a child went soul deep and could no longer be denied.

Zane made a low rough sound as he sought her mouth once more in a tumultuous kiss that left them both breathless. Lesley wasn't sure how much more of this foreplay either of them could take without giving in to their needs. The question had just formed in her mind when the electricity returned. The lamp snapped back on, the force of the light momentarily blinding her.

Zane froze, then swore quietly under his breath. When he eased away from her, Lesley could tell how hard he battled to control his body and his frustration.

"Zane . . ."

He silenced her with a gentle kiss. "A little reality is what we both needed just then. The timing couldn't have been better."

"I want us to make love." It embarrassed her to be so bold, but it was the truth.

"No." His response was flat and hard. "We barely know each other."

"I know enough."

"No," he said again with the same degree of firmness. "You don't know me, and once you do, I can guarantee you won't like the man I am."

Lesley objection was immediate. "I'm crazy about you already. There's something between us, Zane. Don't try to deny it. I felt it the first time we met. You did, too. I realize it sounds crazy, but it's true. I haven't stopped thinking about you. You haven't stopped thinking about me, either. Admit it." She was desperate to have him say the words. When he didn't answer her right away, she said it again, louder this time. "Admit it!"

"Yes," he said forcefully. "But that changes nothing. You're the architect I hired for a remodeling job. I didn't bring you here to satisfy my sexual cravings. Not when that kind of thing can be so easily bought elsewhere."

Lesley gasped. Tears blurred her eyes at the hard edge to his words. She fumbled in her efforts to refasten the pajama top.

"For the love of heaven, Lesley, go back upstairs."

She leapt off the sofa as if someone had urged her with a cattle prod. Certain now that her cheeks had heated to a deep fire engine red, she pressed her hands against her stomach, afraid she might be sick.

"Is it necessary to insult me?" she asked.

His face hardened. "Go upstairs. Please."

"We're going to talk about this in the morning," she insisted, pivoting on her heel. By then she would have reasoned everything out and made sense of what was happening.

"Good night, Lesley."

He couldn't wait to be rid of her, but it wasn't because he didn't want her. Physical evidence claimed otherwise. Nor had he fooled her by claiming another woman would serve him just as well. He wanted her so damn much, it was eating him alive. Furthermore, he seemed to think that once she left the room, his desire for her would slowly dissipate. But he was wrong. Zane wouldn't be able to forget her, not after what had passed between them. He wouldn't be able to forget her any better than she would him.

Upstairs and alone once again, Lesley was convinced she wouldn't be able to return to sleep, but time proved her wrong. Her dreams were filled with Zane.

She woke at eight, feeling refreshed and excited. Lingering in bed, she kept her eyes closed as she held on to the last dredges of her dreams, which had been wonderful.

She pictured herself on the front lawn with Zane and two small children. The four of them appeared deliriously happy.

Had she shared her fantasy with a counselor, Lesley was sure the mental-health professional would suggest she was a candidate for therapy. She'd been with Zane all of two times, and already her mind had conjured up marriage and two children. Talk about projecting one's desires into dreams!

After she'd dressed, Lesley came down the stairs and found Mrs. Applegate in the kitchen.

"Good morning, dearie," the housekeeper greeted brightly. "Did you sleep well?"

"Like a log," Lesley confessed as she poured herself a cup of coffee.

"What would you like for breakfast?"

"Orange juice and toast," Lesley answered absently. "Where's Zane?" She hadn't seen him on her way down the stairs, not that she expected him to be waiting for her, but she'd hoped.

"Mr. Zane had to leave early this morning."

"Oh." She didn't bother to hide her disappointment.

Mrs. Applegate opened the refrigerator and took out a plastic container filled with orange juice. "He asked me to tell you he made several notes on the remodeling plans."

Lesley took a sip of the juice the housekeeper poured for her. "Great. I'll look them over and get back to him directly. You wouldn't happen to know which day would be best for me to stop by, would you?"

"Mr. Zane..."

"Yes?" Lesley prodded.

"He said it would be best if you mailed any changes to him. He wanted me to tell you that his schedule is full, and that he doesn't have any time to meet with you again." The housekeeper looked decidedly uncomfortable. "I know for a fact that isn't true. Mr. Zane has plenty of time. All he thinks about is this project."

Lesley swallowed down the bitter pill of rejection. "I see."

"I'm sorry, dear."

"No, no," Lesley responded with false enthusiasm. "Tell him for me that I'll be happy to mail the plans. And—" she hesitated and set the glass of juice aside "—tell him goodbye for me." Her voice faded to a thin thread of sound.

"It's his leg," Mrs. Applegate insisted. "Some nights it hurts him something fierce, and he isn't himself. He must have had one of his bad nights because he didn't look like he'd been to bed. Be patient with him." The older woman's eyes pleaded with Lesley.

"I can only do what he asks," Lesley said.

"But he doesn't know what he really wants," Mrs. Applegate insisted. "Not when his leg's aching. Now, you listen to me, dearie. Life is much too short to give up so easily."

"Thank you for the hospitality, Mrs. Applegate, but I need to get back to the city." She smiled at the older woman and left the kitchen.

Zane had made his feelings clear. He didn't want to see her again.

Candy Hoffman hated to admit it, but Carl's words had hit their mark. His question about whether she was male or female had hurt far more than she wanted to let on. She'd driven away with a lump in her throat that felt as if it would choke her. But she refused to give Carl the satisfaction of reducing her to tears. By heaven, she was a woman. All right, she didn't dress in fancy frilly things the way some others did, but that didn't make her something she wasn't.

Leave it to Carl Saks to find her weakest link and verbally attack her. Well, she was going to teach that man a lesson. The local Grange was sponsoring a dinner and dance Saturday night and for the first time since her father died and she took over running the feed store, Candy planned on attending.

Although she felt awkward, she put on makeup and dressed to the nines. The skirt, the same one she'd worn in college, was a little snug around the waist, but it still fit. She tried to remember the last time she'd donned it and realized it must have been five or more years back. The black leather boots went real well with the outfit. She hadn't done much with her hair in the past couple of years and was surprised how easily it took to a curling iron.

When she was finished, she squirted on a little perfume and coughed when the fumes got in her nose. She'd had the bottle for ten years or better and was amazed it hadn't completely dried up, although it was about as potent as moonshine.

When Candy pulled into the Grange meeting hall parking area, she looked around at the cars parked in makeshift rows across the thick grass. Although she told herself she wasn't looking for anyone in particular, it wasn't the truth.

She was hoping Carl would be there. She wasn't sure how she felt once she realized he hadn't come. At least his truck wasn't in sight. It was just as well, really. She didn't know if she could look the man in the eye, especially after the insolent way he'd kissed her. Especially after the brazen way in which she'd responded.

Lesley parked her truck and climbed out of the cab. Music blared out from the open doors of the meeting hall, the country-and-western song loud and discordant. The sun had set and cast a golden glow across the horizon in a swan song.

Inhaling a deep breath, she swung her purse strap over her shoulder and headed toward the meeting hall. From the corner of her eye she saw three men sitting on the open tailgate of a truck. They companionably shared a bottle of cheap whiskey. She made a path around them. Not that she expected trouble. In fact, if they asked her to join in, she just might be tempted do it and avoid the stupid social altogether.

The dancing was in full swing when she stepped inside the Grange. She paused in the doorway, feeling out of place, and glanced around. No one appeared to notice that she'd arrived and none of her friends seemed to be around. Rarely had she felt more alone.

"Candy?" Slim Daniels, one of the men who worked at the feed store, strolled past and did a double take. "Is that you?"

"Shut up, Slim."

"My, but you look . . ." He hesitated as if he wasn't sure how she looked. "Pretty," he concluded.

"I said keep your mouth shut," she snapped.

He chuckled and moved on.

Candy made her way to the punch bowl, hoping someone had had the good sense to spike it. She wished now that she'd joined the men on the tailgate. Mrs. Doughtery, a local widow and well in her eighties, was serving up the drink. She smiled sweetly and handed Candy a small glass cup.

Candy hadn't taken more than a swallow when she saw Carl Saks walk through the doorway. He'd come. He'd actually had the audacity to show up. He stood there bold as could be, hands on his hips, looking around. Whether he expected to find her or not, Candy didn't know. When he did see her, she damn sure didn't want him to find her standing next to the punch bowl, looking like a dejected wallflower.

Slim had the misfortune of strolling past. Candy knew a gift horse when she saw one and latched on to his arm. "Dance with me," she instructed.

Slim looked at her as though she'd suggested they mud wrestle together.

"Don't worry, I'm not going to step on your toes."

"Maybe not, but my wife may not take kindly to me dancing with another woman."

"I'll explain everything to Patty later," Candy promised, half dragging him onto the dance floor.

He went with a decided lack of enthusiasm. He shuffled his feet back and forth while Candy threw herself into the dance as if she were auditioning for a Broadway musical. She kicked up her heels, threw her arms in the air and twirled around until the room spun hopelessly.

When the music stopped, she clapped boisterously and kissed Slim's cheek.

Her partner's face flushed red and he whispered, "You better go tell Patty you were the one who insisted on the dance, otherwise I'm gonna be in deep yogurt."

"I said I would," Candy muttered under her breath, and then with a good deal of show, she stepped off the dance floor, greeting people as she went. With her hand over her heart, breathing heavily, she made her way toward Slim's wife. Patty Daniels glared at her husband.

"How about a dance, Candy?"

She looked up to find Derrick Showberg looming over her, preventing her from reaching Slim's wife. Derrick had a problem with booze and was known to have a bad temper. His wife had recently divorced him and claimed spousal abuse. Candy believed the woman.

"It shouldn't be such a hard decision," he said, his eyes holding hers.

Candy froze, not knowing what to do.

"I believe this dance is mine." Carl positioned himself between her and Derrick. "Candy promised it to me earlier. You can dance with her another time."

Derrick's eyes grew hard as flint. "I asked her first."

"I . . . I don't think it's necessary to—"

Carl cut Candy off before she could say anything more. "I said this dance is mine."

"That's too bad," Derrick said, his eyes narrowing, "because Candy seems to have forgotten all about her promise. She prefers to dance with me."

"Candy isn't easily bullied," Carl said evenly. He reached for her hand.

Candy jerked it free. She could see a fight in the making and stepped between the two men, her back to Carl. "I don't think it would be a problem if I had one dance with Derrick," she said, willing to comply if it meant avoiding a scene. Already the three of them had generated interest in the room.

Derrick tossed Carl a triumphant look and steered Candy toward the dance floor. After the fast pace of the previous number, the four-piece local band opted to play a slow dance. Her partner securely wrapped his arms around her waist.

His grip was uncomfortably tight as he snuggled up to her, nuzzling her neck with his nose. Against her will, Candy was forced against his hard, unyielding chest.

"You're lookin' real pretty," he whispered in her ear.

"Thanks," Candy answered without enthusiasm.

"I always said you'd be one hell of a woman if you ever decided to be one."

Candy stiffened. "I beg your pardon?"

"Don't go getting all riled up on me now. I meant it as a compliment." He pressed his cheek to hers and she smelled the liquor on his breath. Great, just great. Derrick had been drinking, and he was a mean drunk.

"You and me have a lot in common, you know."

For the life of her, Candy couldn't think of a solitary thing she shared with Derrick, or that she would ever want to.

"Both of us have got hot blood running through our veins," he explained.

"Hot blood," she repeated. She'd never thought of herself as having a violent temper, nor was she necessarily quick to take offense. The one exception to that was Carl Saks. The man irritated her more than anyone she'd ever known.

"Yeah," Derrick continued, breaking into her concentration. "We're both physical people."

"Physical?" She realized that she was beginning to sound like an echo, but she didn't catch his drift.

"Right. The lovin' between us would be so damn hot, it'd set the sheets on fire."

His words shocked her so much, she snapped back as though he'd physically hit her. "There isn't going to be any lovin' between us, so you'd best get that in your head right now."

Derrick laughed and slid his hand down the small of her spine. Abruptly he brought her back into his embrace. His grip tightened until she was plastered against him. "Don't be so quick to turn me down. It's apparent you're looking for a little action, and I'm downright pleased you chose me over the new fellow in town."

"I didn't choose you." She didn't know where he was getting that message.

His hand dipped farther downward. "Sure you did, sweetheart. Trust me. You and me could have a real good time together. Real good." He cupped his hand over her buttocks and shoved her forward until she felt the thick protrusion in the front of his jeans.

Candy swallowed tightly and frantically glanced around, looking for help. Any port in a storm, as the saying went. Every time she tried to put some distance between herself and Derrick, he took pains to press her more intimately against him. She searched the crowd, looking for someone—anyone—who could rescue her.

She found Slim but he appeared to be involved in a deep conversation with his wife, who didn't seem to be any too happy with him. Biting her lower lip, Candy continued her frantic search until her gaze collided with Carl Saks's. With a single flicker of her lashes she apologized and at the same time asked for his help.

Carl, however, seemed far more interested in drinking a glass of punch. He leaned against the wall, and braced one foot against the floorboard.

She held his look while he raised the cup to his lips, downed the punch in one long swallow and then headed toward the dance floor, easing his way between the couples, moving in her direction.

Candy was so relieved, her knees went weak.

Derrick misinterpreted what was happening. "Hold on, sweetheart," he whispered thickly in her ear. "I'll get us out of here in a minute. If you want, we can go directly to my car. I'm as impatient as you.''

"No," she said with all her strength.

"Okay. If you insist on a bed, we can go to your place, but I don't know if I'm gonna be able to hold off that long. You might have to—''

Carl tapped Derrick on the shoulder. "I'm cutting in.''

Derrick ignored him.

"Let go of me," Candy insisted, struggling.

Derrick stopped dancing and wore a stunned, disbelieving look.

"Let her go," Carl insisted in words so frigid, they made Candy's blood run cold just hearing them.

"Are you going to make me?" Derrick challenged in a loud voice that attracted the attention of the others.

Candy squirmed free, or so she thought. It soon became apparent that Derrick had released her and was looking to prove his claim on her.

The music stopped, and it seemed the entire room focused their attention on the two men and Candy.

"We don't allow any fighting at the Grange," Ronald Bader, a community leader insisted. Ronald made his way across the crowded dance floor.

"Let 'em settle it," someone shouted.

"Take it outside," another advised.

"No," Candy cried, but no one, least of all Carl or Derrick paid her any mind. Both ignored her as if she'd vanished, or was of little consequence.

It seemed everyone inside the Grange hall followed Carl outside. Several of the men raced toward their cars, started their engines and then arranged the vehicles in a wide circle, keeping on the headlights so that a makeshift arena was formed.

"The winner gets Candy," Derrick shouted.

"I refuse to be anyone's prize," she said in a huff, but the only ones who listened appeared to be the other women. Most of them tossed her disparaging looks as if to say this was all her fault.

Candy was willing to admit she'd made a terrible mess of this, but she couldn't think of any way out of it now.

She didn't want to look, but she couldn't keep from watching, either. The two men squared off. Derrick raised his fists and snarled at Carl.

As if this matter were of little concern to him, Carl removed his hat and rolled up his shirtsleeves. From the corner of her eye, Candy saw money being exchanged and realized that several of the locals were placing bets. From the bits of conversation she heard, Carl was the underdog.

She groaned inwardly. Carl didn't have a chance in hell of defeating Derrick. The other man outweighed him by a good fifty pounds, and was at least four inches taller. In addition, Derrick had been drinking and everyone in town knew he was a unscrupulous drunk.

Carl hadn't finished rolling up his sleeves before Derrick threw a punch. The crowd booed. Carl's head snapped back and his nose started to bleed.

Candy gasped and covered her mouth with both hands. "Stop them," she cried. "Someone, please stop them."

No one listened.

Candy watched, amazed at what happened next. Carl wiped the blood from beneath his nose with the back of his hand then stepped toward Derrick.

The bully swung again, and missed.

With four rapid fire punches, Carl sent Derrick to his knees. A cry went up from the crowd and once again Candy saw a fistful of dollars being traded.

Derrick staggered to his feet and shook his head as if to clear his thoughts. Growling, he roared toward Carl. Candy was convinced if he could, Derrick would have killed Carl. She cried out a warning, but none was necessary. Carl easily sidestepped the other man, which only provoked Derrick further. He whirled around and went after Carl with his fists, swinging randomly, punching thin air. Carl deflected each blow and delivered a couple of his own.

Incensed, Derrick raged at him again and fell flat to the ground. When he stood, he had a knife. The steel blade glinted in the light of the cars' headlights.

The crowd gasped, and someone called foul, but neither man paid any heed.

Candy screamed, certain Carl was about to be seriously injured, and all because of her. She'd been so stupid. She should never have come to the dance. She didn't belong here. Didn't belong anywhere.

Carl straightened, wary of the weapon.

Derrick taunted him with the knife, jabbing it at Carl in jest, laughing as if he thought himself clever. A low, disapproving murmur came from the men and women gathered around the two men. One thing was certain, Derrick wasn't making any friends.

Candy wasn't sure how Carl did it, but the next thing she knew, Derrick was on his knees, holding his crotch with both hands and groaning. The knife that he'd used seconds earlier was now in Carl's hands.

It had happened in the blink of an eye. She had seen Carl raise his foot and noted the general direction it traveled. Then the knife flew into the air and seemed to disappear.

The crowd stood in speechless wonder as Carl handed the blade over to Ronald Bader. "I'll trust you to properly dispose of this."

"Yes, sir," Ronald said, looking grateful.

Having dispensed with the weapon, Carl searched the crowd and stopped looking when he found Candy. A path was cleared as he stepped toward her. Everyone seemed to be waiting and watching for what he'd do next.

With the entire Grange community looking on, he walked over to her and reached for her forearm.

"You're coming with me," he said evenly.

How dare he speak to her this way. "I most certainly am not."

"You don't have any choice," he announced in the same cool, measured tone. "I just won you fair and square. From here on out, you're mine."

Chapter Four

"Mornin'," Zane muttered as he sat down to breakfast.

Carl acknowledged him with what was best described as a low growl. Zane noticed the bruise beneath Carl's left eye had started to fade to a sick shade of yellow. He never had learned how Carl came by the injury, but then, he hadn't asked. Carl hadn't been all that anxious to volunteer the information, either.

It used to be that the two of them had plenty to talk about, but recently they'd done little more than snarl at one another. Zane was well aware of the reason for his own general state of disagreement: Lesley.

His mood certainly hadn't improved since the revised plans for the remodeling project had been delivered to the house the day before. He'd taken the blueprints and spread them across the table to study the alterations. As he had been the first time he'd seen the plans, he was awed by what she'd done. With a few strokes of her pen she'd captured the very heart of his home.

She'd captured his heart, as well, Zane reminded himself.

A muscle jerked in his jaw, just thinking about her. It was something he'd vowed he wouldn't do. Proof again of how weak she made him—and weakness wasn't a trait Zane tolerated, least of all in himself.

After the kissing incident in the barn, he had sworn he wouldn't touch her again. At the time, he knew it would be difficult to keep that promise but not impossible.

Within a matter of hours, Lesley had proved him wrong.

The night of the storm, his leg had burned like fire. When he was at his weakest, she'd come to him like a vision. An angel sent by God to torment him. Her hair was mussed, her skin pale and translucent, her eyes soft and loving.

He couldn't believe she was there, and attributed it to a mind fogged with brandy and pain. Then, just when he was convinced she was a figment of his imagination, her hand had joined his to massage the spasming muscle. And her gentleness touched a space deep inside him, a spot he rarely acknowledged and chose not to expose.

Her delicate fragrance reminded him of his grandmother's roses, and when her eyes found his, Zane's body had ached with a longing that was impossible to ignore. In that moment he had to taste her. To hell with the promises he'd made himself. To hell with the consequences. His desire had knotted his insides tighter than the constricting muscle in his leg. He longed to touch her. Longed to taste her. Longed to have her warm and naked beneath him with her arms clinging to his neck while she begged him to make love her, and he rushed to comply.

What he hadn't understood was that those moments had condemned him to a deeper level of hell than what he already suffered. In that brief time with Lesley, his need left him more crippled than the explosion that had nearly cost him his leg.

Even now, Zane was convinced he would have stripped her naked and taken her right there in the library if the electricity hadn't come on.

Talk about the cold light of reality.

Eventually he had found the strength to send her back upstairs. But after she'd left him, he'd been alone to battle his own private demons. As dawn inched its way over the skyline, Zane had made his decision.

Because he was weak, because he didn't have the sense God gave a duck when it came to this woman, there was no help for it. He refused to see her again. Refused to let her dawdle in his thoughts. Refused to care about her.

Only, his dictates hadn't worked any better than his vow not to touch her. Thoughts of Lesley had hounded him from the moment he'd watched her drive away that morning. And the matter hadn't improved with time—not even after a week.

Nothing would change, and he knew it. Not in two weeks. And not in a month.

Zane stood, and slammed his mug on the kitchen table. Coffee sloshed over the edges, staining the place mat.

Mrs. Applegate gasped and placed her hand over her heart. "Is something wrong?"

"Not a damn thing," he said with a snarl. He glared at Carl, half expecting a reaction from his friend, but the former mercenary gave him none.

To irritate him further, Mrs. Applegate chuckled. Apparently she found something amusing. She faced both men and shook her head. "If wise men play the fool, they do it with a vengeance."

Zane hesitated. He didn't like being referred to as a fool, especially by the motherly housekeeper he considered a friend. "What the hell does that mean?" he demanded.

"What do you think it means?" Carl answered, sounding none-too-pleased himself. "You've got a burr up your butt about something. That much is obvious."

"Look who's talking! You haven't said a civil word in days. Not since you showed up with a broken nose and a black eye. What the hell's going on with you?"

"Same as you," Carl snapped. "I've got woman troubles."

"Who said this had anything to do with a woman?" Zane wondered when he'd become that easy to read.

Carl took a long, thoughtful drink of his coffee, then shrugged. "I can't think of anything else that would put both of us in such foul moods, can you?"

"Hell, no."

Carl smiled for the first time in days. "That's what I thought."

Zane stormed out of the kitchen, unreasonably angry and not sure why. He had what he wanted. He had made certain he wouldn't be seeing Lesley again. He should be happy.

He walked into the library, drawn once more to the blueprints that had been delivered the previous day.

The phone rang, and with his eyes still on the plans, he reached for the receiver.

"Zane Ackerman," he said briskly into the mouthpiece.

The person on the other end of the line hesitated. Just when Zane was about to replace the receiver, she spoke. "Zane."

His eyes slammed shut and he gritted his teeth in frustration. He didn't want to talk to Lesley, especially when his defenses were already weakened. The woman wasn't stupid; she knew the power she held over him.

"Did the plans arrive?" she asked hesitantly.

"Yes." He relaxed. So this was the reason for her call. He would assure her everything was fine and be done with it. "I looked them over first thing and couldn't be more pleased."

"I didn't mean to trouble you, but I thought I should check since I'm going out of town for a few days." She sounded as weary and formal as he did himself. "I'm pleased that everything met with your satisfaction."

She was leaving town. Zane nearly choked on the questions that popped into his mind. Ones that were none of his business. Ones that would readily reveal the extent to which she dominated his thoughts.

"Business or pleasure?" he asked before he could stop himself.

"Business. I'm flying to Washington, D.C., this afternoon to meet with a budget committee."

He relaxed, unreasonably relieved to know she wouldn't be lazing on some Caribbean island with a lover. "Have a good trip."

She laughed shakily. "Thanks. I'll try, but I'm not that fond of flying. I know it's ridiculous to worry, seeing that it's the safest means of transportation, but I hate it."

"Will you be flying alone?" There. He'd done it again. Asked a question to which he had no business knowing the answer.

"Not this time. Philip Wong, another architect, is accompanying me."

He hadn't so much as met the other man and already Zane hated him.

"I'm sure Jordan will be in touch with a bid for you soon," Lesley concluded.

The anger inside Zane intensified because he couldn't allow this woman's softness into his life. Because that was what he desperately wanted. Now more than ever.

"Is that everything, then?" He knew he sounded brusque and unfriendly but he needed to get off the phone before she weakened him further.

"Yes." Her soft voice sounded unbelievably hurt.

"Goodbye, Lesley."

"Goodbye." He waited for her to hang up, but neither of them seemed willing to sever the connection.

"Zane."

He strained to hear his name. "What?" he demanded. This was what he got for playing silly mind games with himself.

"Thank you."

She was thanking him? It made no sense when he'd rudely sent her out of his life. "For what?"

"For proving to me that I'm alive. For showing me that I can't ignore my heart. I thought I was happy— I really did. I believed that my job and my interests were all I'd ever need. A friend told me what my real problem is and—'' She stopped abruptly, as though she'd said more than she wanted to already.

"A friend," he repeated.

"It's nothing."

Zane smiled. He could hear the embarrassment in her voice and it intrigued him. "You've come this far—you can't stop now. Tell me what it was your friend said."

"She said . . ." Again Lesley hesitated.

Zane waited, not understanding why he continued to badger her when he should have ended the conversation five minutes earlier. "Yes?"

He heard her soft intake of breath. "Lucy says I've hit the snooze alarm on my biological clock one too many times."

"You want a baby?" he asked before he had time to analyze the question.

Lesley's voice revealed her longing. "More than anything."

A pain he could neither explain nor identify sliced through him.

"I have to go. Goodbye, Zane."

The phone line buzzed in his ear.

Carl had avoided going into town for the past week, and with good reason. Someone was bound to ask him about his black eye.

He suspected most folks in Sleepy Valley had heard about his fight with Derrick Showberg the night of the Grange dance. That much was general knowledge. The son of a bitch had broken his nose, but Showberg wasn't the one responsible for his black eye.

He'd gotten that from Candy Hoffman, the woman who was anything but sweet.

A punch in the eye was his reward for coming to the fair damsel's rescue. He'd have been better off lending a hand to a frustrated porcupine.

One would think Candy would be grateful for his help. She had stood there on the dance floor struggling against that ape, Showberg, tossing Carl pleading glances like greased balls in a fast-pitch baseball game. And what did Carl get for his effort? A nose that was permanently bent out of shape. Well, he could live without her gratitude, that was for sure.

Carl parked the truck and glanced around self-consciously before heading toward Buckwald Pharmacy. When Mrs. Applegate had learned he was driving into town, she'd asked if he'd pick up her prescription for blood pressure medication. Carl could think of no logical reason to refuse, although he didn't relish the thought of someone asking about his black eye.

"Carl."

He tensed at the sound of Candy's voice behind him. He whirled around, none-too-pleased to see her. It was just his luck to run into the little she-devil.

"What the hell do you want?" he demanded.

Everyone in the entire pharmacy turned to stare at him.

"There's no need to yell at me."

Carl decided the best thing to do was ignore her. He'd extended a hand of friendship to her once and had come away with a bloody paw. More the fool if he tried it a second time.

"I'd like to talk to you a moment," she said, sounding all sweet once more. Carl had been buffaloed by her one too many times to be tricked again.

As he recalled, the last time he'd *talked* to her, he'd ended up wearing a beefsteak as an eye patch. There was nothing she could say that would interest him now.

Ignoring her, Carl made his way to the pharmacy counter. "I've come to collect Martha Applegate's prescription."

Elvira Buckwald, whose husband served as the pharmacist, rushed to deliver the order. She seemed as eager to get him out of her establishment as he was to go.

Carl wasn't two steps out the door when Candy shouted, "You're the rudest, most arrogant man I've ever had the displeasure of knowing."

"Stupidest, too," he added, "since you're keeping tabs."

"You asked for that black eye, Carl Saks."

Wonderful. Now the woman had decided to stand in the middle of Main Street and publicly announce that she was the one responsible.

"How dare you think you could win me in a fight!"

Carl groaned. It'd been a joke. Well, it was clear to him the woman didn't have a sense of humor. He should have picked up on that earlier.

"I . . . I didn't mean for that to happen," she admitted, her voice dropping several decibels. "It was a mistake."

Carl snickered. "You're telling me. Getting within a five-mile radius of you is a mistake." Having said that, he took off down the street, anxious to make his escape.

"Would you kindly stop? I have something I want to say," she shouted from behind him.

They'd be shoveling snow on the equator first.

Undeterred by his lack of interest, Candy raced ahead of him, then turned to face him, walking backward. "Would you please listen?"

Since they were already attracting a fair amount of attention, Carl stopped. "What?" he asked, and clenched his hands into fists. He was convinced nothing she had to tell him was going to make any difference. But he knew she was stubborn enough to peck away at him until he did as she asked.

Her shoulders heaved as she caught her breath. The movement was unfortunate because it brought attention to the rounded, fullness of her breasts. Which, despite everything, were probably the finest pair he'd seen on a woman. Okay, so thinking such things would probably be enough to get him arrested. He couldn't help it, he'd always been a breast man.

"I want to apologize," Candy whispered, her eyes avoiding his.

She announced at the top of her lungs that she was the one responsible for my black eye, Carl mused darkly, then apologized for giving it to me in words so low they needed to be dug out of the asphalt. "Okay, you're sorry. As well you should be," he said.

Her mouth thinned.

"Oh, so you aren't sorry?" How like a woman to apologize and not mean a word of it.

"Not about the black eye. You deserved that."

There was no logic to Candy Hoffman and therefore no reason to talk to her. Shaking his head, Carl sidestepped her and continued down the sidewalk.

He'd gone a half a block or more when she pulled the same trick, jogging ahead of him and then whirling around to face him. Her breasts made the same tantalizing up-and-down movement.

"Now what?" he asked icily.

"Please," she said breathlessly, "just hear me out."

The frustration was getting to him. "Is this really necessary?"

"Please, Carl, hear me out."

It wasn't the *please* that convinced him, but the soft, sexy way she'd said his name. He decided he must be getting addle-minded in his old age.

"All right. Just hurry up about it, will you? I got better things to do."

"All right."

For having made such a big deal about it, she didn't seem to know what she wanted to say. "It's about what happened at the dance last week."

"I already guessed that much." He tried to look bored, but if the truth be known, he wasn't opposed to having Candy grovel a little. The way he figured it, she owed him that much.

"I should never have accepted the dance with Derrick in the first place."

"Amen to that."

"I... I don't know why I was so foolish."

If she hadn't figured it out, he had. She'd wanted to thwart him, and by heaven, she'd succeeded. He'd be tarred and feathered before he let her or anyone else at that dance know, but he'd been madder than blazes when she opted to dance with Showberg over him.

"I knew the minute Derrick got me on the dance floor that I'd made a terrible mistake. Then he started making sexual innuendoes and touching me in places he had no right to touch."

Carl hadn't seen that. Showberg had better count his blessings because if he'd seen the ape so much as lay an unwanted hand on Candy, he would have taken delight to dragging the bum outside and beating the bull out of him. Which, as a matter of fact, he had.

Candy rubbed her palms together and appeared to be studying the lines in the sidewalk. "I don't know what I would have done if you hadn't stepped in when you did."

He shrugged, making light of his contribution.

"I mean it, Carl. I'm more grateful than words can say for your help." She glanced up nervously. "I feel bad about the black eye—really I do. It's just that...well..." She hesitated. "We've already gone over that."

"I accept your apology." All right, all right, he was a sucker for a pretty face, and other body parts. Once he'd given Candy the chance, she'd done a good job of making amends.

"You do?" She sounded shocked.

"I'm not an ogre."

She stared at him wide-eyed as if seeing him for the first time in her life. When she realized what she was doing, she quickly closed her mouth and thrust out her arm. "Friends?"

He glared at her proffered hand and sighed, knowing full well she would take all wrong what he was about to say. "I don't mean to offend you, Candy, but I don't think there's a snowball's chance in hell that you and I could ever be friends."

The hurt look that bled into her eyes was painful for Carl to watch. Candy stiffened, withdrew her hand and blinked back tears.

To his surprise, Carl experienced a curious pain all of his own. He didn't mean to hurt her feelings, but this way he was doing them both a service. In time she'd thank him.

Lesley let herself into her high-rise condo and left her briefcase and mail in her small office. Slipping out of her heels, she walked into her living room and literally slumped into her favorite chair. The drapes were open, offering her a sweeping view of the Chicago skyline.

Tossing back her head, she released a deep, pent-up sigh. She was exhausted, both mentally and physically.

Her plane was three hours late due to a runway accident at O'Hara. Two passenger planes had collided. There were said to be fatalities, but she couldn't be sure. The airport itself was a madhouse with emergency vehicles, news reporters and camera crews.

Catching a taxi had been a nightmare.

All Lesley could think about was how pleased she was to be home. Although she loved her job, these business trips had long since lost their appeal. In the beginning they had been fun—even when she was required to fly—but lately, she dreaded every assignment that took her out of town. Plopping her stockinged feet on the ottoman, she crossed her ankles and reached for the television's remote control. She was much too keyed up to go to bed, so she might as well catch the ten o'clock news.

Her phone rang with an urgent discordant sound that broke into the silence like a buzz saw. Groaning, she was tempted to let the answering machine catch it. After four rings, her machine clicked on, but whoever had called, decided not to leave a message.

A half hour later, while Lesley stood in the shower, letting the pulsating spray revive her, she thought she heard the phone ring again.

When she'd finished, she wrapped herself in a thick terry-cloth robe and walked barefoot into her office to check for messages. The red light blinked at her urgently. But when she checked, all that was there was a series of irritating beeps.

Disgruntled, Lesley moved to her kitchen and poured herself a glass of milk. Leaning back against the kitchen counter, she folded one arm around her middle and stared across the condo.

A sadness settled over her. An empty kind of loneliness. A lump formed in her throat, making it grow thick with the need to cry. Although what she had to weep over, Lesley didn't know. How anyone could be surrounded by such luxury and feel this miserable, she couldn't figure out.

A loud peal from the phone startled her. She swallowed a couple of times to help loosen her throat before answering.

"Lesley, thank God." Whoever was calling was deeply relieved.

She frowned. If she didn't know better, she'd say it was Zane on the other end of the line.

"I didn't know what to think. The airlines refused to release the names of the deceased until family had been notified. I've pulled every string I know and couldn't find out a damn thing." He sounded frantic.

"Zane?"

"You're home?"

Lesley nearly laughed at the absurdity of the question. "Of course I'm home."

"You're safe?"

"At the moment, I'm more concerned about you."

"You weren't injured?" The question was brutal with anger.

"In what?" she snapped back. The man was talking in riddles.

"The accident at O'Hara."

"Oh." She'd forgotten about that. "No, I was on another flight."

"But the same airlines," he said, and his voice evened out.

"Yes, but Philip and I caught the later flight." How Zane knew which airline she'd flown, she could only speculate. "You were worried." The words were more statement than question.

He didn't respond, as if doing so would insinuate he cared about her, which was something he'd rather she not know. But she did.

Zane couldn't kiss her with such tenderness if he felt nothing for her. Nor would he have refused to make love to her when she all but threw herself into his arms.

He cared, but for whatever reasons, he'd made the decision to push her out of his life.

And it hadn't been easy for Lesley to accept. But instinctively, she recognized that the harder she pushed, the tighter his resistance would be. And so she'd followed a hands-off policy, and hoped something would happen to change his mind.

"I'm sorry if I woke you." The edge was off his voice and if she heard anything, it was an embarrassed kind of regret.

"How was the trip?" The question was friendly, as if their relationship was on a smooth, even keel.

"Long. Dull. Boring. I'm glad to be home."

"*Did* I wake you?"

"No. I'm generally so wired by the time I arrive home that sleep is impossible."

The line was silent, and for a moment, Lesley feared she was talking into thin air.

"When I heard about the accident," Zane said, his words low and barely discernible, "I didn't know what to think. You'd mentioned how afraid you were to fly—" He stopped abruptly, as though he regretted admitting this much.

"I *am* afraid," she admitted softly.

"It happens," he said, his voice stiffening. "The things we fear most. Sometimes I believe we bring them upon ourselves." He stopped and inhaled sharply. "Lesley, I apologize. I've made a first-class fool of myself, and as Mrs. Applegate mentioned not long ago, I've done so with a vengeance. Forgive me, please."

"It isn't a problem. Good night, Zane."

"Good night."

The conversation was over and all at once Lesley knew she would be able to sleep, and when she did, she knew her night would be filled with happy dreams.

A week later, Lesley arrived at Jordan and Molly Larabee's with a bouquet of fresh-cut flowers and a bottle of her favorite white wine.

"Lesley." Molly greeted her at the door and kissed her on the cheek. Nine-month-old Ian was riding his mother's waist, swinging a set of large, plastic keys. "I'm so pleased you could come," Molly added, stepping aside to let her in.

"Are you kidding?" Lesley joked. "A home-cooked dinner that I don't have to fuss with myself? It sounds heavenly."

"Jordan's barbecuing," Molly explained, bouncing the baby on her hip. "Thank goodness. I've got my hands full with the kids."

"Let me help," Lesley said, following Jordan's wife into the kitchen. She placed the wine in the refrigerator to cool and left the flowers on the counter.

Molly eyed the baby iris. "That wasn't necessary, you know."

"I'd bribe you with a lot more than wine and flowers to hold Ian." Lesley put her arms out to the toddler, who liked the idea. He stretched his arms toward Lesley.

"Lesley, you're wearing silk," Molly warned. "He's teething and likely to drool all over you."

"She's accustomed to having men drool all over her," Jordan said, stepping into the kitchen.

Lesley laughed at the absurdity of such a statement, but it was nice to have her ego flattered, especially since it had taken such a beating of late.

Ian slipped his chubby legs around her waist and reached for her dangly earrings.

It had been awkward being friends with Molly in the beginning. But Lesley had soon gotten over that. Seeing that she often worked with Jordan, it was important that the two women reach an agreement.

Soon after Bethany was born, Lesley and Molly had sat down and talked openly. Their discussion had revolved around Lesley's short relationship with Jordan.

Secure in her husband's love, Molly had gone out of her way to put Lesley at ease. In the three years since Jordan and Molly had reunited, Lesley considered the contractor's wife one of her best friends.

Lesley pulled out a kitchen chair and crossed her legs, letting Ian ride on the end of her foot while holding on to his plump arms. She was so involved in playing with the little boy that she didn't notice someone else had entered the kitchen. When she caught sight of a figure standing just inside the sliding glass door, she glanced up, a ready smile in place, waiting for an introduction.

Her foot went still. So did her heart. "Zane."

"Hello, Lesley. It's good to see you again."

Good to see you again. She wasn't sure what was required of her. Ian squalled in protest, not wanting the fun to end. Lesley felt disoriented, as if she'd been on a carnival ride that had spun around so many times, she'd lost her equilibrium.

She lifted Ian from her foot and cuddled him close, almost as though she needed the baby to insulate her from the pain caused by seeing Zane.

"What are you doing here?" She didn't realize how rude the question was until she voiced it. "I mean...I didn't know anyone else had been invited."

"We're starting work on Zane's house this week," Jordan announced as he reached inside the refrigerator for a plate piled high with thick porterhouse steaks.

"So soon?" Lesley's gaze traveled from Jordan to Zane.

"The sooner the better, don't you think?" Jordan commented.

"Of course." Lesley couldn't keep her muddled thinking straight. Had she known Zane had been invited, she would have mentally prepared herself for the meeting. To happen upon him like this completely knocked the breath out of her.

"Mommy, Mommy, bring Aunt Lesley to see," Bethany called from the backyard.

"Jordan built her a playhouse," Molly explained to Lesley as she carried an hors d'oeuvre plate outside to the picnic table.

"This I've got to see." Taking Ian with her, Lesley followed Molly outside, but it wasn't her friend's craftsmanship that interested her.

"Why didn't you tell me?" Lesley whispered the minute the two women were alone.

"About Zane coming?"

"Yes," Lesley said in hushed tones.

"I didn't know. We invited him more than a week ago and he refused." Molly took Ian from Lesley and placed him in the high chair set up on the patio. "Then, out of the blue, he called and asked if the invitation was still open. We were thrilled. It isn't often that we see him. This is the first time since his—" she paused, and lowered her voice "—since his accident. From what Jordan said, Zane rarely leaves Sleepy Valley." She glanced toward Zane, and Molly's eyes saddened. "He's a good man, Lesley. A very good man. He risked his life for Jordan and me."

Lesley didn't understand, but wasn't given the opportunity to question Molly further.

"Come look, come look," Bethany insisted, taking Lesley's hand and pulling her toward the one-room playhouse. Lesley had seen apartments built with less flourish. Jordan had outdone himself.

She allowed the three-year-old to show her around.

"Bethany," her mother called, "it's time to get ready for dinner."

The little girl raced toward her mother.

Zane joined Lesley, his gaze following Jordan's daughter. "What you said the other day about children . . . Did you mean it?"

"Yes," she answered, her heart pounding. "I want it all."

"All?"

"Marriage, children, a home."

"I see." Zane's gaze held hers for several long moments before he turned and walked away.

Chapter Five

Zane accepted early on that the remodeling project would be a damned nuisance, but he hadn't realized exactly how much it would disrupt his life. A constant parade of workers walked in and out of his house. Sawdust and noise became incessant irritants.

Mrs. Applegate was in an uproar in an effort to protect her precious territory. When she wasn't yelling at the workers to be careful about one thing or another, she was feeding them freshly baked cookies. Zane wasn't sure this was such a good idea. He didn't want to give the construction crew any incentive to take longer than absolutely necessary.

Zane did his best to stay out of the workers' way, but his home and his life were no longer his own. As the month of May progressed, he wondered what had ever possessed him to make expensive and drastic changes in a home he wouldn't live long enough to enjoy.

As had become his habit each morning, Zane walked out to the stable to saddle Arabesque, his black gelding. This hour of peace and quiet had become his sanity.

Carl was in the barn, busy working the tractor's engine. Zane entered the barn and heard his friend cursing under his breath.

"Having problems?" Zane asked.

Carl looked up and frowned. "Not really." He reached for the rag tucked in his hip pocket, and strolled toward Zane. "Have you got a minute?"

"Sure." Zane glanced at his watch. Lesley was due to arrive at ten, but he'd be back in plenty of time to meet her. It had been almost two weeks since the night of the Larabees' dinner, and in that time, Zane had given serious thought to his relationship with Lesley. Asking her to review the progress on the house was little more than an excuse to see her again.

Carl seemed to find it necessary to clean his hands. He concentrated on wiping away the grease before he asked, "Would you object if I went back to ordering supplies from Hoffman's?"

The question surprised Zane, and he could tell Carl was uncomfortable asking it. "I told you before those decisions are yours to make. I trust you to get the best price, and beyond that, it doesn't matter to me."

"Good." Carl turned back to work on the tractor and reached for a wrench.

Because he couldn't resist, Zane asked, "I thought you didn't want anything more to do with that Hoffman woman?"

"I don't," Carl insisted heatedly, tossing a wrench back into his toolbox. It landed with a clang. "But I feel I might have been a bit hasty earlier, pulling our business."

"The decision is yours," Zane reminded him.

Carl nodded abruptly. "I should mention something else. I found a piece of property that interests me, north of Sleepy Valley."

Zane knew Carl would eventually move on, but he hated to have him leave. Up to this point, their arrangement had been loose. Carl lived in the guest house, and helped with the horses. As it was, he'd taken on several other responsibilities. It would be difficult to find someone to replace him.

"It's got fifty acres and plenty of open space."

Carl was a natural with horses. When they'd talked about what they'd do when they gave up soldiering, Carl had mentioned his desire to raise the world's finest Arabians.

"It sounds ideal."

Carl leaned against the side of the small tractor and crossed his arms. "The place needs a lot of work, but I'm not afraid of that. The way I figure, it could be another year or more before I'm able to start buying my stock."

Carl never had been one to show a lot of enthusiasm, but Zane could see his friend was excited about this property. He was slow and meticulous, traits which had come in handy over the years. He'd make the decision about the land the way he did everything else—in his own time and in his own way.

"I haven't made any decisions yet, but I figured I should mention it."

"Let me know what you decide."

"I will," Carl said, and turned back to the tractor.

*   *   *

Carl made an excuse to drive into town later that morning. He was honest enough to admit he had no real reason, other than to see Candy Hoffman.

It'd been over two weeks since he'd last talked to her, and frankly, he missed their sparring matches. His life had been downright dull without crossing swords with that little hellcat. If the truth be known, he enjoyed their verbal battles.

Chuckling to himself, Carl recalled how her face would get all red, starting with her neck. The hot color would work its way up her face until the tops of her ears looked as if they were on fire. There was no way in hell that woman could hide her feelings. She was a hot-tempered wench, and by heaven, he'd missed her.

By the time he pulled up in front of the feed store, Carl was in a good humor. His mood improved when he found Candy in the back of the store, sassy as always, issuing orders like a drill sergeant.

She stopped midsentence when she saw him standing there. "What do you want?" she barked.

Something was different about her. It took Carl a minute to put his finger on it. She wore makeup and her hair was curled. Why, she looked as good as she had the night of the dance.

"Hello to you, too," he said with a slow, lackadaisical smile.

Candy hugged the clipboard against her bosom as if she thought it would protect her.

"Answer my question. What do you want?" she asked again.

"I've had a change of heart," he said, and reached for the folded slip of paper inside his shirt pocket.

She eyed him warily. "A change of heart about what?"

"Giving you my business. I've got a number of items listed here that I'd like delivered." He handed her the slip, expecting her to be grateful. Instead, she stared at him with a shocked look.

"I thought you said..." she mumbled, then stiffened. "As I recall, you claimed it'd be impossible for the two of us to be friends."

"I don't have to like you to do business with you, do I?" The instant the words slipped out of his mouth, Carl realized he'd said the wrong thing. Furthermore, it wasn't what he meant. He did like Candy—that was the crux of the problem.

The red started creeping up her neck, and he realized that this time he'd jumped into it with both feet.

She thrust his list back at him as if it were diseased. "I don't need your business, Mr. Saks, especially in light of the fact—"

"I didn't mean that the way it sounded." Already he knew it was too late. Candy wasn't in any mood to listen to reason. The list fell to the floor. Carl would have bent over and retrieved it, but when Candy was in this mood, it was conducive to his health to keep his eyes trained on her.

"Perhaps it would be best if you left my store now," she said, glaring ferociously at him.

"You're kicking me out?" Carl couldn't believe his ears. The woman had the audacity to actually oust him over a simple misunderstanding.

"You're damn right I'm kicking you out." She raised her arm and pointed toward the front door, as though he wasn't smart enough to find his own way.

Apparently he wasn't moving fast enough to suit her purposes, because she shoved him hard enough for him to damn near lose his balance.

"Get out," she shouted, "and stay out."

Carl was tempted to stand his ground, and would have, if not for one simple factor. Tears glistened in Candy's eyes.

Tears.

Muttering under his breath, he left, but he didn't feel good about it. In fact, he was downright miserable. This wasn't what he intended. On the drive over, he'd been thinking that they might stop in at the local café and chat over coffee. He was hoping they would find common ground, talk matters out. He'd have liked it if they could have reached an understanding.

Instead, everything had blown up in his face.

The problem, Carl realized, was that women were irrational creatures and he didn't know how to deal with them. Both angry and frustrated, he removed his hat and slapped it against his thigh.

He knew it wouldn't be long before the word got around town that Candy Hoffman had tossed him out of her feed store. This woman was a real detriment to his reputation.

Across the street from where he'd parked the truck was a flower store. Carl stood next to his pickup and stared at it for several minutes. Women were said to be partial to flowers. Maybe he should let a bunch of roses do the talking for him. With that thought in mind, he jogged between traffic and walked over to stand in front of the window.

Glancing over his shoulder, he remembered the way Candy's eyes had glistened. It seemed a bunch of those pretty yellow daisies with the black centers were a small price to pay for having unintentionally offended her.

The bell over the door chimed as he walked inside.

"Can I help you?" The proprietor, a middle-aged woman with kind eyes, greeted him.

Carl peeled a hundred dollars off his money clip. "Do you know Candy Hoffman?"

"Of course. She took over the feed store when her father died a few years back."

"Send her as many flowers as this will cover." He set the money on the counter and started to walk away.

"You can't leave," the woman called.

"I can't?"

"I need to know what kind of flowers you want? How many? And what about the card?"

"A card?" Carl paused, his hand on the doorknob. "Do you need extra for that?"

"No...no." The woman was clearly flustered. "Generally, a card is enclosed. Candy will want to know who sent her the flowers."

Carl hesitated, then shook his head. "She'll figure it out without any card. As for which kind and how many, I'll leave that up to you." He hurried out the door before someone recognized him.

The minute Lesley turned into the long driveway that led to Zane's home, she experienced a keen sense of homecoming. The feeling was similar to what she'd felt on her first trip to his property. The house reached out to her with wide, open arms. Unfortunately, the proprietor wouldn't.

Zane's invitation had come as a welcome surprise. Lesley had given up any and all attempts to understand Zane. Whenever they were together, the attraction between them was so powerful, it affected everyone around them. The air seemed to spark with electricity. People seemed to stop and wait for something to happen between Zane and her.

Dinner with their friends had been an ordeal for them both. Zane couldn't seem to take his eyes off her. She was guilty of staring at him, as well. After a while, as rude as it sounded, Lesley felt that Molly and Jordan were an intrusion.

Watching Zane with the Larabees' two children had brought tears to her eyes. Bethany was naturally curious about his scar. Zane had held the three-year-old and allowed her to trace her small finger down the side of his face.

With limitless patience, he answered the questions Lesley had been afraid to ask. A very bad man had done that to him and, no, it didn't hurt. Not anymore.

Lesley had been captivated, studying Zane with Bethany and Ian. He seemed to be equally enthralled watching her with the children. Being with Bethany and Ian reminded her of how badly she longed for a child herself.

Lesley sighed and shoved the memories from her mind. Instead, she forced herself to focus her attention on Zane's home.

It was apparent that the remodeling project was in full swing. The place hummed with activity. A stack of building supplies lined one side of the lawn. A van and a pickup truck were parked in front, and a series of men purposely strolled in and out of the house.

Lesley parked away from the construction vehicles and climbed out of the car. No sooner had her car door closed than Mrs. Applegate stepped onto the porch and waved.

"Oh, my. You're a sight for sore eyes, dearie."

Lesley hugged the older woman.

"Have you ever seen a bigger mess in all your life?" the housekeeper asked under her breath.

"It won't take long. I promise," Lesley said, hoping to comfort Zane's housekeeper.

"All this mess has got Mr. Zane unsettled."

"Is Zane around?" She was right on time, and disappointed he wasn't here to greet her himself.

"Mr. Zane's on the phone. I'm sure he'll be available any minute. Come into the kitchen with me. I just made a pitcher of lemonade." Mrs. Applegate glanced around and then lowered her voice. "He misses you."

"I'm sure that isn't true."

"Mark my words, dearie. That man needs a woman in his life. And the one he wants is you."

A stocky fellow, wearing a hard hat, stopped them. "I don't suppose you've got any more of those oatmeal cookies left, do you?"

"Of course," Mrs. Applegate said, beaming with pride. "I'll get you a plate when I bring out the lemonade." The minute the man was out of sight, the housekeeper whispered, "I swear these men are eating us out of house and home. The big one over there ate a dozen of my oatmeal cookies in one sitting just this morning."

Lesley had trouble hiding a smile. Mrs. Applegate was in her element now that she had someone who appreciated her home-baked goods.

"Lesley." The doors to the library glided open and Zane stepped out. As it always seemed to happen, Lesley couldn't take her eyes off him. Her skin felt hot and sensitive just being with him. It embarrassed and frustrated her that he could make her want him with just a look.

"What do you think?" Zane asked, making a sweeping gesture toward the remodeling effort.

"I bet you feel like you should be wearing a hard hat."

A saw buzzed loudly, interrupting their conversation. "Let's go outside," Zane suggested, leading the way.

As they made their way across the thick lawn, she realized that his limp wasn't as noticeable. Katydids buzzed at their feet and the scent of cut grass and sunshine followed them.

Zane led her to the viewpoint she'd found on her first visit. The sweeping panorama of Lake Michigan held such exquisite beauty that it stole her breath. To enjoy it with Zane standing beside her heightened her enjoyment tenfold.

"My grandfather used to stand here."

"I thought you said it was your grandmother's favorite spot."

"It was, but after she died, my grandfather came here often. He was never the same after Grandma was gone. It seemed like a part of him died with her."

"How long did he live afterward?" Her own grandparents had died within nine months of each other. Lesley had been ten at the time, but she remembered the tremendous sense of loss she'd experienced with their passing.

"I don't know," Zane said. He walked over to the concrete bench and sat down. Lesley joined him. He reached for her hand, the first time that he'd voluntarily touched her in weeks. "My parents divorced shortly after that summer and my mother didn't want me to have anything more to do with my father's family.

"We moved to California, and adopted another name. I didn't realize it at the time, but she'd kidnapped me. But then, I don't think any eleven-year-old fully understands what happens when his parents stop loving each other."

His hand tightened, painfully pinching her fingers, but Lesley was convinced he was unaware of what he was doing. Gradually the pressure decreased.

"I never saw him again," he said with a heavy bitterness weighing his voice.

"Your grandfather?"

"Or my father."

This explained so much. Zane had been ripped from the arms of a loving father, taken from the only family he'd ever known and thrust into a new life with a new name, understanding nothing.

"Did your mother remarry?"

He stiffened when she mentioned his mother. "No." The lone word answered more than her question. With it came the knowledge that it was unlikely he'd allow another woman into his life. Whatever had happened between Zane and his mother had left him wary and embittered.

"The happiest days of my life were spent at this house," he said thoughtfully. "It's why I found it. Why I bought it. And why I decided to restore it to its former grandeur."

All at once Zane stood, as if he couldn't bear to sit any longer. "Are you interested in going out on the lake?"

Her heart leapt with excitement. "I'd love it."

"There's a stairway that leads down to the water. My sailboat's docked there." He hesitated and glanced her way, his eyes smiling. "I should warn you, however, that it's been a good long time since I've sailed."

"We'll manage," she assured him.

His gaze held hers for an elongated moment. "I imagine we will."

The tractor engine was giving Carl nothing but trouble. He'd spent the better part of the morning fussing over it, to no avail. It was getting to the point where he was going to have to read the manual. Which only went to prove the sorry state of his mind. He'd like to blame Candy Hoffman for that, too.

His back ached from leaning over the blasted tractor, and his mood had been sour ever since he'd gotten back from town that morning. He tossed the wrench back inside the toolbox, and pressed his hand against the small of his back. What he needed was a break.

He picked up the sandwich Mrs. Applegate had set out for his lunch and carried it to his house. One thing was sure, he wasn't going to get any peace and quiet at the big house. A man couldn't hear himself think for all the racket going on in there.

Zane wasn't around, either. Earlier, Mrs. Applegate had said something about him being with Lesley. That left a man to wonder. Zane and Lesley . . . Well, more power to him. Even a casual observer could tell which way the wind blew with those two. Although Carl couldn't help but wonder what Zane intended to do about Schuyler.

Together, he and Zane had stood over the graves of Dan and Dave, their two comrades, and Zane had sworn he'd get even. He meant to do it too. Zane intended to go after Schuyler himself.

A chill raced down Carl's spine at the thought of the terrorist. Schuyler was responsible for Zane's injuries and for the death of two good friends and countless innocents.

Carl sat at his kitchen table, the manual for the tractor engine open in front of him. A knock sounded at his front door.

"Who the hell is it?" he demanded. Rarely did anyone disturb him here, which was just the way he wanted to keep it.

"Candy Hoffman."

Carl damned near upset the table as he bolted upright. Candy Hoffman!

He decided to play it cool, and took his own sweet time getting to the door. She'd probably come to personally thank him for the flowers, and to apologize for the way she'd treated him earlier. As well she should.

He opened the door, but Candy wasn't wearing a smile the way he assumed she would be. In fact, from the sour look she gave him, he wondered if she'd gotten his flowers. He almost asked, and probably would have if she hadn't shoved a clipboard into his stomach.

"Sign here," she demanded.

"For what?" he asked just as irritably.

"Someone has to sign for the delivery."

"What delivery?"

She looked at him as though he should have his intelligence tested. "I seem to recall that you personally stepped into the shop and gave me a list this morning."

"Oh." It didn't take him long to recover. "I thought you said you didn't want my business."

"You changed your mind, didn't you?" She didn't wait for him to respond. "I changed mine. You want these supplies or don't you?"

"All right, all right," he grumbled under his breath. There wasn't a pen with the board so he walked over and pulled open the kitchen drawer, searching for one.

"Thank you for the flowers."

He almost didn't hear her—the words were so low. He looked up and their eyes met. Candy didn't look the way she normally did, with her eyes snapping at him, just waiting to leap on some comment he made. Her eyes were all soft and feminine. Tender like. His stomach clenched the way it had when she'd told him about Showberg touching her in places she didn't want to be touched.

With difficulty, he pulled his gaze away from her. Because of the effect she had on him, his voice was sharp and unfriendly when he spoke. "I didn't mean to upset you this morning."

"Are you saying you want to be friends, Carl Saks?" she asked defiantly. She held herself stiff, almost as if she were afraid of his answer.

The frustration in Carl reached the boiling point. "You don't get it, do you?" he said angrily. "You just don't get it."

"Get what?" she asked just as loudly.

The best way to tell her was to give her an example. He tossed the clipboard aside and started toward her, cutting the distance between them in four strides.

A lesser woman would have hightailed it in a dead run. And the way he was feeling right then, it might have been better if Candy had.

She didn't fight him when he wrapped his arm around her waist and hauled her forcefully against him. He knew when he kissed her that his mouth was hungry and hard. For weeks, he'd been thinking of doing just this. Ever since the first time in the stable. He'd burned with a hungry need to touch her, to make love to her. What angered him the most was that Candy hadn't a clue how he felt about her.

Nothing he'd said or did eased the fire. It threatened now to burn out of control.

He pulled her blouse free of her waistband, all the while kissing her. She made soft, incoherent noises, as their mouths twisted against each other and their tongues dueled.

Their kisses grew deeper, more intense and physically demanding. Carl had expected her to scratch his eyes out before now, but she gave as good as she got, clinging to him, whimpering and moaning. Knowing she was as hot for him as he was for her, fueled his actions.

His objective was her beautiful breasts. The need to feel them, to taste them, dominated every thought and movement. He wanted to take her directly into his bedroom, but couldn't make himself break off the kiss.

Somehow, with the both of them struggling, they were able to free her of her shirt and bra. When her breasts spilled into his open hands, the effect was so damn potent that Carl's knees went weak.

Candy rotated the lower half of her body against him and Carl groaned aloud. Much more of this and he wasn't going to last long enough to make it to the bed.

With little care, he jerked open the snap of her jeans and shoved them down over her buttocks. His need was urgent as he quickly released his own zipper. By then, he was so aroused, he had difficulty freeing his manhood.

Candy intended to help him, he guessed, but when her hands closed around him, it nearly drove him over the brink.

The only thing to do was to give her a taste of her own medicine. Bracing her against the wall, he slid his finger between her legs. Candy released a moaning whimper at the intimate contact.

"Please . . . oh, Carl, please."

"What is it you want?"

"You . . . please. Give me you."

Carl groaned out loud as he brought his manhood more forcefully against her. "Like this?"

"Yes."

He glanced over his shoulder, wondering how long it would take to get her to his bed. Too long, he decided. Too damn long.

She moved against him, and this time he wasn't able to choke back a cry. The woman had been driving him crazy for weeks. He couldn't wait. His entry was slow and deliberate, the pleasure so keen, he clamped his eyes shut and bared his teeth in an effort to keep from exploding right then.

With her back braced against the wall, Candy wrapped her legs around his waist. When he found the strength to move, she met each of his thrusts with a lusty cry. She moved against him, panting and sobbing.

Mindless with need, Carl clamped his hands on her hips, driving into her hard and fast until the pulsing release freed him, much sooner than what he wanted. But it had lasted far longer than he dreamed.

His breathing was harsh and heavy as he braced his forehead against hers. "Now you know," he choked out between gasps for breath.

"Know?"

"Why we can't be friends."

His words were met with a shocked kind of silence. The next thing he knew, he was forcefully shoved away from her. They both would have fallen to the floor, if Carl hadn't caught himself.

Before he could figure out what was wrong, Candy slammed her fist against his shoulder. She didn't do him any harm, but she must have hurt her fist because she let out a yelp.

"What's wrong now?" he demanded.

"Just leave me alone." She twisted herself free of his embrace.

It took him longer than it should have to realize she was crying. It was much more than tears brightening her eyes. Full-scale sobs shook her shoulders and caused her to tremble so bad, she could barely stand upright. Her head hung low as she struggled to right her clothes.

"What did I say this time?" he asked.

She shook her head, her hands trembling so hard, she couldn't fasten her blouse. Carl figured he didn't have any choice but to help her, although heaven knew it wasn't what he wanted. He'd been so hot for her that he hadn't taken time to pay proper attention to her breasts.

He cupped the side of her face. "Whatever I said that was so terrible, I'm sorry."

She glanced up at him, and again he had the feeling she was afraid to trust him.

"You're good, baby, real good." His nose nuzzled her neck, and he planted a series of delicate kisses there. "I can't remember the last time I enjoyed a bout of sex more."

"Sex!" She roared the one word at him, then plowed her fist into his stomach so hard, she knocked the breath clean out of him. He doubled over, more stunned than hurt, and watched helplessly as she raced out of his house, slamming the door in her wake.

The sailboat sliced through the deep green water of Lake Michigan. Lesley loved the feel of the swift breeze that whipped her hair about her face. She closed her eyes and turned her head skyward, soaking in the brilliant sunshine.

"This is fabulous," she shouted to Zane, who manned the helm. He smiled back at her. It wasn't a real smile, but as close as he got to revealing his pleasure.

When he stretched out his arm, in silent invitation for her to join him, Lesley slipped naturally into his embrace. "It's a perfect day for this."

"My grandfather used to take me out with him," Zane told her. "I loved it then.... I'd forgotten how much." His arm tightened around her shoulders.

He seemed unnaturally quiet after that. Once or twice Lesley attempted conversation, but it soon became evident that Zane had no interest in chitchat. His eyes remained dark and serious, and he had the look of a man who had something on his mind.

As if reading her thoughts, he spoke. "I've been doing a lot of thinking lately."

She didn't probe, knowing he'd reveal his thoughts when it suited him.

"Your comment about wanting children has stayed with me."

She'd assumed this had something to do with the house. "Children?" Often in the past weeks, she'd wondered what madness had possessed her to mention her desire for a family. It embarrassed her.

"You'd be a good mother, Lesley."

"I'd like to think so." She knew she sounded breathless, but he'd taken her by surprise.

"You're patient and gentle and you possess a kind heart."

She thought of all the good qualities she'd seen in him, but knew he wasn't interested in hearing about himself.

"There comes a time in a man's life when he thinks about the future."

He must have given the subject a good deal of thought following his injuries, she realized.

"Sort of a biological clock for men?" she joked.

He chuckled softly. "In a manner of speaking, I suppose you're right. When I die . . ."

"But that's a good many years from now."

He didn't respond.

"I've given some thought to what my legacy will be, and realized there'll be nothing in this world to say I've lived. Nothing to say that I've loved or that I've cared. You, on the other hand, will leave a mark with or without a family."

"You mean the buildings I've designed?"

"Yes. But I won't have anything to pass on. I have no family, no children, and I've come to realize those things are important to me."

He made death sound imminent, as if he gave the subject much thought, and that distressed her. "We certainly have gotten onto a dark subject."

"We haven't known each other long," he said as if she hadn't spoken. "But I've felt a physical and emotional connection with you from the first. I've tried to reason it away, tried to pretend it doesn't exist, but that hasn't worked."

Lesley lowered her head. "I've felt it, too."

"You want a child and I want an heir."

Lesley held her breath, then whispered the question. "What are you saying?"

"I'm asking you to marry me, Lesley."

Chapter Six

"Marriage," Lesley repeated softly. The word echoed in her mind as if Zane had shouted it against a canyon wall. Each time it bounced back, she wondered if his proposal was a figment of her imagination. Zane had all but pushed her out of his life; now he was asking her to be a major part of it.

"There's a good deal to be said in favor of the two of us marrying," he continued. "I'm a wealthy man. You'll never need to worry about finances again."

Lesley bristled. "There's more than money involved in such a commitment." It irritated her that he would consider his fortune as his greatest asset.

"You don't need to give me your answer right away."

She wanted to ask him about love, but her thoughts remained scrambled and confused. It would seem that Zane must hold some tenderness for her, otherwise he wouldn't have proposed. Not unless he had an ulterior motive. And she couldn't imagine what that would be.

When it came to defining her feelings for Zane, Lesley wasn't entirely sure what she felt. Love was difficult to explain. Over the years she'd come to recognize that it had little to do with beauty, passion or romance.

Three years earlier, she'd thought she was in love with Jordan Larabee. Only later, after he'd reunited with Molly, did she understand that her feelings for him were linked with her almost despairing desire for a husband.

"Do you love me?" She wasn't sure what made her blurt out the question when she was fully aware of the answer.

Zane didn't hesitate. "I figured you would ask me about that, and it's a fair question. One that deserves an answer. But frankly, I don't know what to tell you."

Lesley appreciated what it had cost him to be honest, however painful it was for her to hear. It would be a simple matter to justify her response if Zane were to confess an undying need for her. But he hadn't mentioned his feelings toward her, almost as if they were of little importance.

"I know little of love, little of softness," he added. "I enjoy your company, and for me that's enough. As for the physical aspect of our relationship...well, that speaks for itself, doesn't it?"

"It's true we seem to be sexually compatible, but that isn't love."

"Not entirely," he was quick to agree.

"My mother loves cats, but my dad is more of a dog person." she said, thinking off the top of her head, and wondering if she could define her needs to Zane. "Several years ago Dad bought her a calico, which Mom promptly named Whiskers. My mother was crazy over that silly cat. She lavished Whiskers with attention and love. Then Whiskers developed leukemia and had to be put to sleep. My dad was the one who went to the vet's office with Mom. When she wept, he held her and comforted her. That's love, Zane."

"You want me to buy you a cat?"

"No." Men could be so obtuse. "I'm trying to tell you that I'm not looking for some deep, heart-wrenching confession of undying love from you. Love isn't glamorous. Sometimes it isn't even pretty. It's holding my hand at a movie. It's helping me to the bathroom when I'm sick. It's reminding me to wear a sweater when it's cold outside."

He studied her, as if the concept were something new to him, and she could tell that he was doing his best to understand.

"You want me to be with you all the time?"

"No." It was all she could do to keep from groaning with frustration. "Love embraces without restricting. I would never change who you are, Zane. I want to encourage you to do the things you want, and at the same time count on your emotional support for my own endeavors."

Leaning forward, he braced his elbows against his knees and was silent for several long moments. "I don't know that I can do all the things you're asking."

Her heart fell.

"But," he added thoughtfully, "it wouldn't be because I don't care about you. I'd need help, is all. To me, love is a decision. I could love you or I couldn't, depending on any number of factors. If we married and produced a child ..."

"Children."

He didn't contradict her, but she noticed he didn't amend his statement, either. "...All the things you're saying would fall naturally into place, wouldn't they?"

"Perhaps." Lesley remained confused. She was excited and at the same time frightened. Zane was offering her a chance for the kind of life she'd always yearned for, but he was quick to point out his own limitations in the husband department.

"Would you mind kissing me?" she asked.

Always before, when he'd brought her into his arms, their kisses had been hot and hungry, their need urgent, the kisses both compulsive and explosive.

Now, the gentleness with which his mouth claimed hers brought tears to Lesley's eyes. His lips, moist and tender, slid over hers in an unhurried exercise, coaxing a response from her.

Lesley opened to him and his tongue swept her mouth in slow, sensual strokes.

When the kiss ended, she planted her hand over her heart and kept her eyes closed.

"The loving would be very good between us," he said in what she was sure was an effort to sway her decision. "Very good."

Lesley couldn't doubt him. Rarely had she felt more physically compatible with a man. But there was far more to marriage than lovemaking, yet at the same time Zane was right not to discount their attraction for each other.

"You said earlier that love isn't passion," he reminded her.

Too weak from his kisses to answer verbally, she nodded.

"But it has its place. Marry me, Lesley, and give us both what we want." He nudged her head aside and dropped soft kisses along the underside of her jaw.

Goose bumps skittered across her skin as he deftly used his tongue to excite her, licking at her senses, eating away at her doubts. When he was touching her like this, it was too hard to think.

"I ... I don't know what to do," she admitted with a soft moan.

"You don't have to answer me right away. Mull it over. Mull it over long and hard. But when you've made your decision, be certain, because there'll be no going back for either of us."

Zane was convinced he'd blundered this proposal. He wasn't the kind of man who pussyfooted around a subject. He'd invited Lesley to come sailing with him for the sole purpose of asking her to be his wife. It had seemed simple enough when he'd come up with the idea, but when the time came, he found himself wavering, and not for the more obvious reasons.

Lesley wanted children; she'd told him so herself. Zane wanted an heir. The importance of a child hadn't hit him until he fully contemplated his own demise. As a mercenary, he faced death with each assignment. He was good at what he did—damn good—and he knew it. But he was not invincible. When he waged war, he went into battle knowing the odds. He didn't make mistakes.

Call it vanity. Call it ego. Call him a fool. But for the first time in his life, Zane owned a part of his family's history. He possessed a small piece of himself to hand down to the next generation. Since moving to Sleepy Valley, he found it vital to know that when he left this life, a part of himself would live on.

The house had played a role in his decision to propose to Lesley. She loved the place almost as much as he did. Her appreciation and deep regard for his grandparents' home had shown in her ideas for the renovation. She'd captured the very essence of his home and her designs had brought out the natural beauty in each and every room.

But it was more than that.

Zane recalled how she'd instinctively located the viewpoint that had meant so much to his grandmother. Before he'd told her, she'd been intuitively drawn to the one spot on the entire estate that held special meaning.

After being with Lesley, Zane felt as if God, in His almighty wisdom, had offered one last chance. He'd sent a beautiful, magnificent woman into Zane's life at the eleventh hour. Zane believed Lesley was his destiny.

Yet, when the moment came to propose, his throat had closed up and his tongue had felt three times its normal size. What he had assumed would be easy became difficult.

The reason was simple. Marriage to him would be grossly unfair to Lesley. If he died in the confrontation with Schuyler—and he fully anticipated that with his physical limitations he would—then Lesley would be left to rear their child alone. True, he'd leave her a wealthy widow, but she'd been the first one to point out that financial security wasn't everything.

If he did manage to survive, she'd be saddled with an ugly beast of a husband. With his leg in as bad a shape as it was, he would always be crippled. No amount of cosmetic surgery would make him the husband she deserved.

Lesley left soon after they docked the sailboat, promising that she would have an answer for him within the next couple of days.

Zane watched her drive away. He had two minds in the matter. He wanted her, more now that when he'd originally come up with the idea. At the same time, he realized he was a selfish bastard.

So what else was new.

First thing the following morning, Candy phoned in sick to the feed store. But it wasn't a flu bug that afflicted her. No, her malady was one of the heart. Every time she thought about the scandalous way she'd behaved with Carl Saks, her cheeks burned with mortification. Her first inclination had been to blame Carl for what happened. But her conscience refused to let her forget that she'd been a willing participant in the exchange.

A thick lump formed in her throat and she battled back tears. She dressed in an old pair of threadbare jeans and an ugly T-shirt that was ready for the rag bin. Her choice of wardrobe was a good indication of her state of mind.

She had to stop thinking about their lovemaking and get on with her life. With a determined effort, she made herself a cup of tea and popped a piece of bread into the toaster. As she waited for the tea bag to steep, she realized that was what she'd been doing all night: steeping her mind with regrets.

How could she have been so stupid as to let her relationship with Carl dissolve to this level? She found it difficult to answer her own question. She didn't know how she would ever be able to look the man in the face again. Carl nothing—she found she couldn't look at herself in a mirror and not experience a sick kind of dread.

That matter of seeing Carl again was simply solved. She wouldn't. She would sever him from her life as quickly and as cleanly as she could.

The tea and toast helped revive her physically, and she felt a little better. Well enough to consider stopping off and checking on the store. She was about to do just that when the doorbell chimed. Her mistake was answering the door without first checking to see who was on the other side.

Carl.

Candy attempted to slam the door closed, but his foot prevented her from doing so.

"What's the matter, Candy?" he asked, and his mouth formed a dark, sardonic twist. "If I didn't know better, I'd say you weren't pleased to see me."

"Leave me alone," she cried, and pressed the full weight of her body against the door in an effort to escape him. She should have known better. Her valiant struggle did nothing.

"We need to talk," Carl insisted.

"I have nothing more to say to you." The bravado she'd managed with him earlier was gone. She glared at him, but was mortified when all she could muster was a humiliating bout of tears. Her eyes filled with moisture and his figure blurred. "Leave me alone, or I'll be forced to call the authorities."

To embarrass her further, Carl chuckled and called her bluff. "No you won't, and we both know why."

She squared her shoulders, but kept her eyes trained away from his face. "I don't have anything to say to you."

"Invite me in."

The man had nerve—she'd say that for him. "Not on your life."

"Fine, if that's what you want. I'll stand out here on your front porch and half the neighborhood will hear how we were so hot for each other, we damn near burned down Zane's guest house."

Mortified, Candy reached for Carl's elbow and jerked him inside her living room. "All right," she cried in frustration. "Say whatever it is you have to say and then get out."

"Aren't you going to do the polite thing and ask me if I want any coffee first?"

She ground her teeth. "No."

He looked around at the compact living room and glanced toward the kitchen. "Nice place you've got here."

"Carl, please, don't make this any more awkward than it already is." She hated the soft desperation she heard in her voice and bit her lower lip.

Without waiting for her to suggest he make himself comfortable, Carl sat down on her sofa. He reclined, making himself at home, and propped his ankle on his knee as though he had all the time in the world.

Reluctantly, Candy claimed a seat across from him, sitting so close to the end of the cushion, she was in danger of falling butt first onto the carpet.

Since she had little choice in the matter, she'd listen to what he had to say, cut her losses and pray to the highest heavenly authority that she'd never see the man again.

The tension in the silence that followed was palpable.

"How are you?" Carl asked gently. Carl Saks was a lot of things, but gentle wasn't one of them. To the best of her knowledge, it was the first time he'd ever treated anyone with tenderness.

"I stopped off at the store and they said you'd phoned in sick," he elaborated.

"I'm hunky-dory. What do you think?" she returned flippantly, not willing to be taken in by this gentle side of him.

"I was pretty rough with you. I never intended—"

"Please," she cried and covered her face with both hands. "Don't talk about *it*."

"That's exactly why I'm here...."

"Don't you understand?" she shouted, glaring at him. "It should never have happened...I don't know why it did. I've never...I'm not like that... I'm not on the Pill...." She stopped because her throat became thick with tears and it was impossible for her to speak coherently.

The silence was punctuated with her efforts to breath normally and hide her distress.

Candy whipped the hair out of her face. "I don't want to see you again. We're not good for each other...we seem to bring out the worst in one another."

"I disagree."

"Please, Carl." The desperation was back in spades. "I won't ever ask anything more of you."

"Why don't you want to see me again?"

It actually sounded as though she'd hurt his feelings.

"We're bad for each other. We have this love-hate relationship." She counted off the reasons on her finger. "Tell me, exactly where will our relationship go from here?" Tears marked tracks down the side of her face and she swiped them away with the back of her hand.

"It seems to me we've got the perfect relationship."

"Perfect?" She couldn't believe her ears.

"Sure. We already know we're compatible physically."

"What you're saying is that we can just cut to the chase and do away with everything else."

"Yes." He sounded downright jubilant.

Candy reached for the decorator pillow at the end of the sofa and hurled it at him. He caught it easily between his hands and seemed at a complete loss when she dissolved into sobs.

Her anger revived her enough to leap to her feet and point the way to the door. "Get out of my house."

"Why?" He seemed sincerely shocked by her response.

"I don't want *sex* with you."

The edge of his mouth lifted upward in a slow, easy smile. "I bet I can prove otherwise."

If she'd had something convenient, she would have thrown that at him, too, but she was running out of pillows and patience. "Didn't you hear anything I just said? What kind of woman do you think I am? Please, Carl . . . just go." She buried her face in her hands and refused to look at him.

"You're overreacting."

"Please," she pleaded, willing him to leave.

"We need to talk this out."

"There's nothing more to say." She glanced up at him, hoping he would realize that she was at the end of her rope.

After a tense moment, he stood and walked all the way to her front door. Abruptly he turned around to face her. "What about if we started dating?"

She groaned. Didn't the man know the definition of the word *no?*

"We could make a fresh start." He closed the distance between them. He studied her, his eyes dark and probing. "It's not a bad idea, you know."

She reached for a tissue inside her pants pocket and loudly blew her nose. "What about, you know...what happened?"

"We'll put the incident behind us."

Candy didn't know if starting over would be possible now, but she teetered, tempted more than she thought possible by the prospect. It was difficult to refuse him when he was this gentle. She could deal with his anger—thrived on it. But she had no defense against this side of him.

"You can send me away," he continued, "and I'd go because that was what you wanted. But at some point we'd run into each other again, and it'd be the way it always is between us."

Undecided, Candy nibbled on her lower lip.

"Sparks would fly and soon we'd be spatting over one thing or another."

He was beginning to make sense and that was a dangerous sign.

"Before we knew it, we'd end up falling into the same trap as before, so hot for each other that we'd—"

"I get the picture," she said bluntly. Still Candy hesitated, unsure if what he said made sense or if she wanted to believe him so badly that she was willing to agree to any terms.

"Hello, Candy Hoffman," he said, and offered her his hand. "I understand you own and operate the local feed store. I'm Carl Saks."

She studied his open hand as if that would tell her what she needed to know. It was worth a shot, she decided, then squared her shoulders and slipped her hand inside of his. "Hello, Carl."

They studied each other for several moments, and a tentative smile touched Carl's mouth. "I hope you won't think I'm being too forward if I invite you to dinner with me on such short acquaintance."

"Dinner?"

"I understand that Bluebeard's serves up a fine prime rib and all the trimmings."

"When?" Of all the questions she should have asked, "when" was probably the one least important.

"Tomorrow night. Hell, tonight."

"Tomorrow," she agreed.

His smile was full-blown now. "I'll pick you up at six."

"I'll be ready." She'd never been the blushing, reticent type, but she felt that way now. Unsure of herself, of Carl, yet yearning for the opportunity to start again.

"You won't regret this," he promised, and then as if to seal their agreement, he leaned forward and kissed her with a hunger that hurled her senses straight into outer space.

A day passed and Zane didn't hear from Lesley. Her decision on whether to marry him wouldn't be easy, he realized, but he hoped he'd persuaded her.

Not until after she'd left did he remember they hadn't kissed, except briefly the one time when she'd asked it of him. To not influence her with the strong physical attraction they shared hadn't been a conscious decision, but it was a wise one.

If she did suffer regrets—and she would, if she chose to marry him—he didn't want her to look back and assume she'd been coerced into agreeing.

In an effort to get out from under the constant irritation of the construction workers, Zane decided to take Arabesque for an afternoon ride.

His nerves were on edge and he realized his nervousness was due to Lesley. He wanted her answer, one way or the other, so he could move forward.

If she turned down his proposal, then he'd make plans to go after Schuyler as soon as the remodeling was complete. His scheme for vengeance against the terrorist was progressing beautifully. Zane's first line of attack had been against Schuyler's finances. He wanted to hurt him where it would affect him most, and since Schuyler assumed Zane was dead, he hadn't a clue how it was happening. If by chance Lesley did agree to marry him, then Zane would hold off on his revenge until after he was certain Lesley was pregnant.

Arabesque's sleek neck appeared over the stall door when Zane entered the barn. He reached inside his pocket for a sugar cube and fed it to him while he gently spoke to the gelding.

Carl, who was breaking up a bale of hay with a pitchfork, glanced up from the other end of the barn. "Howdy," he called, looking pleased with himself.

"You seem to be in a chipper mood."

"I am," Carl returned.

"Any particular reason?"

His friend leaned against the pitchfork and Zane swore he wore a grin as wide the Mississippi River. "I've got an important dinner date coming up."

Zane assumed it had something to do with the property Carl had mentioned purchasing not long ago.

His friend returned to the task at hand, whistling a Roger Whittaker ballad as he pitched hay.

It didn't take Zane long to saddle Arabesque. The gelding was in the mood for a run. Generally he held him back, but not this afternoon.

After a brisk workout, Zane looked longingly toward the beach. The path down was a series of steep switchbacks that demanded all his skill as a rider. Because of the time and attention it entailed, Zane rarely rode Arabesque on the shore.

He was three-quarters of the way down the steep hillside when he heard voices. His view was blocked by a large boulder, but he didn't need to see the trespassers to know that they were there.

Being careful not to attract their attention, Zane painstakingly wound his way farther down the hillside. As he neared the rock, he was more able to make out the words.

"What if we get caught?"

"He never comes down this way. He's not going to catch us."

Whoever it was didn't sound to be more than nine or ten. Boys, Zane decided, looking to make trouble.

"He'd kill us if he ever found us."

"No, he wouldn't."

"He's been in prison. I heard my mom talking on the phone with Mrs. Wilson and she said he got those scars in a fight while in a federal penitentiary. She said he was up for murder."

"Murder," the other two repeated.

Murder. This was news to Zane. He knew that the locals thought him a monster, but this was the first time he'd heard he was fresh from the slammer.

"I bet he escaped and that the law's looking for him."

"Yeah."

Zane couldn't resist it any longer. With Arabesque's head held high, tail swishing, Zane led his gelding from behind the huge rock.

Three boys stared up at him, their eyes wide with fear, their mouths gaping open. "This is private property," Zane announced in his sternest voice. "I suggest you leave before I decide to press charges and have you thrown in jail."

Two took off running so fast, their tennis shoes kicked up small rocks. The third boy, the smallest, scampered up the hill. His foot hit a loose rock and he lost his footing. With what must have been a shot of frantic fear mingled with alarm, the lad rolled down the rocky landscape and landed no more than a few feet from Arabesque's prancing hoofs.

The wind seemed to have been knocked out of him because he doubled up and didn't seem to be able to breathe.

Zane climbed down off his gelding and knelt down beside the boy. "Take small breaths," he advised calmly. "And don't panic. The pain will pass in a moment." He removed his own jacket and tucked it under the boy's small head.

"It's gonna hurt like hell, but it won't last long."

The boy's chest heaved and he panted. His eyes were incredibly round as he stared up at Zane.

"Don't worry, son, I'm not going to do you harm."

As soon as he was physically able, the youngster sat upright. It was apparent by the way he immediately edged away from Zane that he didn't trust him.

"I said I wouldn't hurt you," Zane repeated. "Is anything broken?"

Another boy appeared around the corner, and with a yell Tarzan would have envied, he hurled himself at Zane. "Leave my brother alone."

Zane captured the older boy and tucked him under his arm. The child kicked and screamed, legs and arms flailing out wildly as he lashed out in a desperate effort to save his younger brother from certain death. The boy on the ground leapt to his feet and kicked at Zane's bad leg with all his might.

Zane bit off a groan at the stabbing pain that shot up his thigh. With his free arm, he circled the younger boy's waist and lifted him off the ground. Now he had two squirming boys to contend with.

It didn't take either one of them long to expend their energy. The oldest gave out first. The youngest stopped soon afterward, and glanced up at Zane with a look that revealed both anger and terror.

"Are you going to eat us?" the youngest boy asked.

Zane burst out laughing, the sound echoing with the wind.

"That was a stupid question," his older brother admonished. "Of course he isn't going to eat us."

"Don't be so hasty, boys. You look like mighty tasty fare." Then because he was having such fun, Zane reared back his head and shouted. "Fee, fie, fo, fum, I smell the blood of an Englishman."

"You won't hurt us," the older of the two announced. "Tommy got away and he'll be back with the police."

"Good," Zane said calmly. "I'd like to talk to them myself. It seems the three of you were on private property. I'd be well within my rights to have you penalized."

"What's "penalized" mean?" the younger whispered out of the corner of his mouth.

The older of the pair ignored his brother.

"It means you'd be in big trouble with your parents," Zane explained.

"Maybe we'd be better off if he ate us."

Zane howled. Nothing had struck him so funny in years. He released both boys, certain they'd made good their escape.

Neither one did as he expected. Instead, they stared up at him as if they'd never seen a man laugh before.

"You're not a monster," the youngest stated.

"Don't be so sure." For effect, he raised his arms and roared. Both boys cowered, but stood their ground.

"I guess I can't fool you," Zane said as he walked back to Arabesque. He reached for the reins and swung up into the saddle with graceful ease. The leather creaked as the gelding accepted his weight.

"What are your names?" he asked.

"Eddie," the oldest said.

"Dennis."

"Last name."

"Smith," Eddie said quickly, too quickly. "Eddie and Dennis Smith."

"Try again, and this time I want the truth."

"Glasser," Dennis confessed. "Our dad works for the gas company."

"Mom's a homemaker."

"You tell your parents for me that they've raised a fine pair of boys. But it's not a good idea to come down here to this stretch of beach without getting my permission first, understand?"

Both boys nodded simultaneously.

"Goodbye, boys."

"Goodbye." They turned and took off running, their young legs kicking up rock and sand in their rush to find their friend and tell him of their adventure.

With a smile, Zane finished his ride. Welcoming the freedom, Arabesque took off down the beach in a full gallop. A motion from the corner of Zane's eye caught his attention. He looked up toward his property and to his delight discovered Lesley standing at the viewpoint. She was dressed in red, and when she realized he'd seen her, she waved.

He returned the gesture. Lesley had made her decision. Because of the distance, Zane couldn't read her expression. His first inclination was to assume she'd decided to accept his proposal. Then he realized she was the type who would face him either way.

With a flick of the reins, Zane urged Arabesque up the hill. Instead of taking the switchback, Zane drove the gelding up the steep slope, using both the talent of his animal and his skill as a rider to make the vertical climb.

By the time he reached the top, Arabesque was slick with sweat. When he returned his gelding to the barn, Carl volunteered to cool him down.

"Give him a handful of extra oats," Zane instructed. Then, because he was anxious to see Lesley, he left.

He found her hurrying across the front lawn. He didn't want to appear overly eager, and at the same time his heart felt like an air hammer pounding holes into his chest. Her decision shouldn't matter this much, but it did.

He wanted a son. A boy like the ones he'd happened upon while on the beach. A child who would fight against impossible odds to save his brother. One with backbone and honor.

They met halfway across the yard. He searched her face, thinking he might read the answer in her eyes.

"I've made my decision," she said, looking confused and uncertain. Her eyes seemed red rimmed, and he couldn't think of a single reason for her to weep.

"I was convinced we'd both be making a mistake if we married."

Disappointment zeroed in on Zane like a hawk narrowing in on a field mouse. He should have realized it would take more than the promise of financial security to tempt a beautiful woman like Lesley to marry a monster like him.

"Perhaps if we spent more time getting to know each other.... Surely you realize we're barely more than acquaintances."

"No." He hadn't the time nor the patience for a lengthy courtship. "If you agree to be my wife, we'll be married by the end of the month."

"Not this month?"

"This month," he countered. But she'd already decided otherwise, so it shouldn't matter.

Lesley lowered her gaze. "I saw you just now with those two boys, and saw how good you were with them, and I understand now. I feel . . ."

What the Glasser boys had to do with this Zane didn't know.

"I'd made my decision," she whispered, and it sounded very much like she was on the verge of tears. "Damn you, Zane Ackerman, damn you." She fell into his arms, sobbing for no reason that he could ascertain.

When her emotion was spent, he eased her away from him enough to look at her face, which was blotchy and red. "Lesley, what's wrong?"

"Me, that's what's wrong. I want this. I want a family. I guess what I'm saying is that I'll marry you."

This seemed to be a day for celebrating. Because it was impossible to hide his happiness, his arms surrounded Lesley's waist and he whirled her around, shouting at the top of his lungs.

Chapter Seven

Carl was determined to do everything right on his date with Candy. He didn't stop to analyze why it was so damned important that he mend fences with the little hellcat. Frankly, he feared he wouldn't like the answer.

When he first started dealing with her at the feed store, he actively disliked her. The woman drove him nuts. He'd never liked bossy, opinionated women, especially ones who seemed to think they could compete in a man's world, and did. Nor did he appreciate the way she tried to disguise the fact she was a woman. With breasts a cover model would envy, it seemed a downright shame for her to walk around in such an unflattering wardrobe.

Then out of the blue, Candy started dressing and acting like a woman. He recalled the night of the Grange dance. He'd walked in and spied her across the room, talking with one of the men who worked at the feed store. She was beautiful. He couldn't take his eyes off her—what a difference a little makeup and a skirt could make. From that moment forward, Carl hadn't been able to stop thinking about making love to her.

After their explosive lovemaking, Carl had assumed that the hot need would be satisfied. But it hadn't worked that way. Instead of satisfying him, their one time together had created a need for more. His thoughts were dominated with the question of how long he'd have to wait to have her again. He grew aroused just thinking about the way it'd been between them. Explosive. Urgent. Volatile. Exciting.

If all it took was a box of chocolates, a bunch of red roses and dinner at the finest restaurant in town to get back into Candy's good graces, then he'd consider it well worth the effort.

Carl dressed in his best shirt and jacket and even splashed on a shot of rum-scented cologne. He would have liked to talk about what was happening between him and Candy, but the only person he could think to discuss it with was Zane. But then Carl figured his friend didn't know anything more about courting a woman than he did himself.

In the past, women were a luxury neither man could afford. Relationships were out of the question. That wasn't to say Carl didn't have experience. He had plenty of that, but his partners rarely lasted more than one night.

He left the house whistling and arrived at Candy's promptly at six. She opened the door and he was struck dumb. Carl swore he'd never seen a more beautiful woman in his life. And he'd seen his share, with and without clothes.

THE EDITOR'S "THANK YOU" FREE GIFTS INCLUDE:

▶ Four BRAND-NEW romance novels
▶ A Porcelain Trinket Box

PLACE
FREE GIFT
SEAL
HERE

YES! I have placed my Editor's "thank you" seal in the space provided above. Please send me 4 free books and a Porcelain Trinket Box. I understand I am under no obligation to purchase any books, as explained on the back and on the opposite page.

335 CIS AW7M (C-SIL-SE-01/96)

NAME

ADDRESS   **APT.**

CITY   **PROVINCE**   **POSTAL CODE**

Thank you!

DETACH AND MAIL CARD TODAY!

THE SILHOUETTE READER SERVICE™: HERE'S HOW IT WORKS

Accepting free books places you under no obligation to buy anything. You may keep the books and gift and return the shipping statement marked "cancel". If you do not cancel, about a month later we will send you 6 additional novels, and bill you just $3.21 each plus 25¢ delivery and GST*. That's the complete price, and—compared to cover prices of $4.25 each—quite a bargain! You may cancel at any time, but if you choose to continue, every month we'll send you 6 more books, which you may either purchase at the discount price...or return at our expense and cancel your subscription.

*Terms and prices subject to change without notice. Canadian residents add applicable provincial taxes and GST.

If offer card is missing write to: Silhouette Reader Service, P.O. Box 609, Fort Erie, Ontario L2A 5X3

0195619199-L2A5X3-BR01

CDMA Member

SILHOUETTE READER SERVICE
PO BOX 609
FORT ERIE, ONT
L2A 9Z9

MAIL ≫ POSTE
Canada Post Corporation / Société canadienne des postes
Postage paid   Port payé
if mailed in Canada   si posté au Canada
Business   Réponse
Reply   d'affaires
0195619199   01

Candy wore a long black skirt that closely hugged her hips, revealing long, sleek graceful lines. She had on the same black boots as the night of the dance, and the soft white V-neck sweater that drew his attention to the gentle swell of her breasts.

Carl's mouth went dry just looking at her. He wasn't sure how he was going to go the entire evening without his tongue dangling out of the side of his mouth, wanting her the way he did. He must have stared too long because she laughed softly and stepped aside.

"Hello, Carl."

"Here." He thrust the bouquet of roses and a box of chocolates at her, unable to be rid of either fast enough. He felt like a damn fool as it was.

"How sweet." Candy closed her eyes, sniffed the roses and smiled gently. "Thank you, Carl."

He shrugged, wishing now he'd bought out the entire flower store since she seemed to be so fond of the roses.

"The chocolates were the best Buckwald Pharmacy had." He would have preferred giving her Belgian ones, but he'd need to drive into Chicago to find those.

"I'm sure they're delicious."

"Are you ready to go?" He checked his watch. He hadn't made reservations, but he didn't know how long he was going to be able to keep from touching her. Especially when it was just the two of them alone.

"I thought we'd have a glass of wine first...that is, if you don't mind."

"Sure," he said, swallowing tightly. Wine. He should of thought of that himself. The next time they went out, he'd remember to include a bottle of wine along with the chocolates and flowers.

Candy walked into the kitchen and he followed her. His gaze fell on her hips and the way they gently swayed from one side to the other. The movement was more sexually provocative than if she'd purposely set out to seduce him. With effort, he forced his gaze away, and slowly counted to fifteen in an effort to rein in his growing need for her.

Already his mind had calculated the problems in removing her skirt and had decided the best way to deal with it was to bunch it around her waist and save both them both time and effort. Briefly he wondered how long it would take them to find the bedroom. They hadn't made it there the first time and he was determined to be more civilized about their lovemaking the next.

Candy opened the refrigerator, bent forward and brought out the wine. He might have imagined it, but it seemed to him she wiggled her rear at him. His loins tightened to painful proportions.

Carl was in trouble and he knew it. "Maybe wine wouldn't be such a good idea after all," he blurted out. Sweat formed on his upper lip and he was getting hotter by the minute. When she glanced his way, surprise written on her features, he added, "Being that I'm driving and all."

"Of course, I should have thought of that."

Carl had been drinking hard liquor for years and one glass of Chablis wasn't going to impair his ability to operate an automobile. But it could greatly weaken his resolve—and he was determined to behave like a gentleman, even if it killed him. At this rate it just might. "Shall we go," he asked.

Bluebeard's was by far the best restaurant in town, but by no means fancy. Once they arrived, the hostess, a local woman Carl recognized from the Grange dance, seated them in a corner booth. Candy greeted her by name. Hilda, he thought, but it didn't matter. The only woman he had eyes for was Candy.

He was greatly relieved now that they were in public. Candy tempted him beyond reason. The only way he could guarantee his behavior was when they weren't alone.

"The blackened prime rib is delicious," Candy said, glancing at him over the top of the menu.

Her recommendation was good enough for him. He closed his menu and set it aside. Candy couldn't seem to make up her mind. He watched as her gaze slid across one side of the plastic-coated menu and then the other. She glanced his way and offered him a nervous smile.

In the end they both ordered the blackened prime rib. Dinner proved to be an enjoyable experience. Once he was able to ignore how much he wanted Candy physically, Carl discovered she was a knowledgeable horsewoman. She seemed surprised by his own expertise in the area.

When he mentioned the property he was thinking of purchasing, Candy brightened.

"That sounds like the Gaudette place."

The name sounded familiar to Carl. "The house needs plenty of work, and the barn is shot. I'd need to tear it down and build another one."

"I don't think anyone's lived there in ten years or more."

"Twelve, according to the real estate agent." Before long, Carl found himself telling her about his ideas for remodeling the place. He used the back of a paper napkin to draw a diagram of the property and where he'd considered placing the barn in relation to the house and other outbuildings.

Candy asked a number of thought-provoking questions and fervently disagreed with his plan for cutting down a grove of hundred-year-old apple trees.

"With a bit of pruning and care, those trees could easily produce again."

Carl had thought of that himself, but he didn't have the time or energy to hassle with the fruit. He'd have his hands full with everything else that needed to be accomplished on the property.

On the drive back to Candy's place, Carl started to worry. Thus far, everything had gone real well, and he didn't want to ruin it by doing or saying something stupid now.

"It's still early," Candy announced when he pulled up in front of her house. "Would you like to come in for a cup of coffee?"

He'd like nothing better, but it wasn't coffee that interested him. He wavered, and involuntarily his gaze lowered to her breasts. For most of the evening he'd done an admirable job of avoiding temptation, but his control was slipping. . . .

"I make a decent cup of coffee."

His eyes snapped back to her. Candy was saying she wanted him, otherwise she wouldn't be so eager to get him inside her house. He damn near leapt out of the truck in his hurry to give her what they both wanted. The way he figured, she couldn't come right out and tell him her feelings. Women liked to think it was the man's idea. Fine. He'd leap through hoops if that's what it took to get her to bed.

It seemed to require an eternity for her to unlock the front door. She'd set her purse aside and started toward the kitchen when Carl caught her by the arm. She looked back at him, her eyes revealing her surprise.

"I don't want coffee and neither do you."

She came without resistance into his embrace. When his mouth settled over hers, she gave a soft little moan of welcome.

This was heaven, Carl decided, as the hunger exploded between them. More by luck than any skill, he managed to find the sofa. He literally fell into it, taking Candy with him. With a soft cry of surprise, she landed with a solid whoop into his lap.

Carl laughed and directed her mouth back to his. The kiss was slow and deep and the excitement began to pound inside of him. Their kissing had always been good, but never quite this good.

But it wasn't enough to satisfy Carl for long. It seemed a downright shame to waste time with it when there were other more pressing matters that needed attending.

The hook of her bra was in the back and he made a mental note to ask her to wear the type that latched in the front. It frustrated him no end to have to fuss with it.

When he managed to unfasten her bra, he slipped his hand inside her T-shirt and cupped her full breast. It delighted and amazed him the way her nipple puckered into a hard peak at his touch.

"Carl..."

"In a minute, baby." Holding her fullness between his hands, his lips closed over the hardened peak and he sucked gently. Her breasts tightened and swelled.

"Carl . . . no more."

"You don't mean that." He tried to kiss her, to convince her otherwise, but she twisted her head away.

"I do mean it." She braced her forehead against his shoulder and drew in several deep breaths. "Either we stop now or we'll end up making love."

Wasn't that the point? Carl tightened his jaw, fighting back his own physical needs. All right, if that was the way she wanted to play the game, then fine, he was a patient man.

"This is only our first date, remember?" she asked in a voice that trembled with need.

Carl was comforted with the knowledge that she was having as difficult a time putting an end to their love play as he. But it was damn little consolation. What irritated him most was that he had no one to blame for this but himself. He was the one who'd come up with the brilliant idea of the two of them starting over again.

One thing was certain, many more dates that ended like this and it would be a kindness to take him out to pasture and shoot him.

Lesley's head was spinning. From the moment she'd agreed to marry Zane, her life hadn't been the same. In addition to completing her current work commitments, she had been expected to organize and plan a wedding to take place in less than three weeks' time.

She'd only seen Zane twice in the past fourteen days, and when they were together, their time was filled with decision making.

What she couldn't understand was the urgency Zane seemed to feel about their marrying quickly. It was almost as though he feared she'd change her mind.

She wouldn't. Now that the decision had been made, Lesley had absolute confidence that she was doing the right thing. From that first day when she'd driven to the house, she'd experienced a spiritual bonding with Zane. But when she announced to her parents that she was marrying Zane, they were concerned that she could be making a terrible mistake.

Her mother had repeated the old wives' tales—marry in haste, repent in leisure—to convince her she shouldn't marry Zane, at least not until she knew him better. Her father, the ever-logical attorney, had raised several legitimate concerns. He asked that she consider these questions before going ahead with the wedding.

Then her parents had met Zane.

The three of them had driven out to the house on a Sunday afternoon. Lesley knew Zane and her family were nervous about the meeting.

Lesley had done her best to prepare her parents, explaining the extent of Zane's injuries. Nevertheless, her mother had gasped softly when she first saw him. Her father, his eyes dark with doubt, insisted that he and Zane speak privately. It both embarrassed and hurt Lesley that the two people she trusted most in this world doubted her judgment.

As it turned out, Zane had easily won over both her parents. She never learned exactly what was said between the two men, but her father came out of the meeting, singing Zane's praises. By the end of the day, Zane had charmed her mother.

Two days before the wedding, Lesley was finishing up the last project when Molly Larabee arrived at her office unannounced. "I'm taking you to lunch," Jordan's wife insisted.

Lesley sat back in her chair and relaxed. She was as ready as she'd ever be for the wedding. It felt as if the whole world had been tossed upside down in the past weeks. Everything was crazy, but it was a wonderful kind of crazy. She didn't know of a single other bride who worried about government contracts two days before her wedding. A luncheon escape sounded perfect.

"Where are you taking me?" she asked, a willing captive.

"There's a new French restaurant I thought we'd try," Molly said. "The kids are spending the day with their grandfather and I'm free until five. I figured we'd let our hair down and have some fun."

After the hectic pace of the past few days, Lesley could do with a relaxing afternoon.

"Just think, next week at this time you'll be an old married woman."

It was hard for Lesley to believe, but the mere thought produced a bubble of happiness. "People think I'm nuts, you know. Marrying a man I barely know."

"I'd marry a man like Zane in a heartbeat," Molly announced. "Don't listen to what anyone says. Listen to your heart." She placed her open hand over her own breast. "I did that when Jordan and I reunited. In some ways Zane was responsible for that."

"Zane?"

"I never told you how I met Zane, did I?"

"No." Naturally Lesley was curious.

Molly rolled a chair toward Lesley's desk. "Do you remember when Jordan came to get me out of Manuka?"

"Of course." Lesley wasn't likely to forget that time. Jordan had gone to find Molly to ask for a divorce so he'd be free to marry her. Instead, he'd ended up arriving in the middle of a political revolution and rescuing Molly.

Days before his departure, the government of Manuka had been overthrown. Rebel soldiers closed in around the medical compound where Molly served as a nurse.

In an effort to save his wife's life, Jordan had been shot, and carried the scars of his adventure to this day.

"Zane was the leader of the men Jordan hired to get me out."

Leader of the men Jordan hired. The words rang like church bells, clanging around inside Lesley's head. Her surprise must have shown because Molly elaborated.

"You didn't know that?"

"No."

"We were trapped inside the medical compound. Zane and his men were caught in the cross fire and were forced to leave Jordan and me behind.

"I'll never forget when I saw that helicopter lift off without us. I was certain Jordan and I were doomed. There was no escape left. It would only be a matter of hours before the rebels overpowered the men defending the compound."

"Zane saved your lives."

"Yes. Not only did he come back for us, but he managed to keep the rebels from overtaking our weak defenses."

Zane had been a mercenary.

If Lesley hadn't already been sitting down, she would have required a chair. Not wanting to appear even more of a fool than she already was, she smiled and said nothing.

"That night in the jungle, convinced we were both about to die, Jordan and I made our peace about losing Jeff. You see, I'd never told him how sorry I was."

"Sorry?" Lesley knew the death of her infant son had devastated Molly.

"*Guilty* is a better word," Molly elaborated. "As a medical professional, I assumed I should've been able to do something to have prevented Jeff's death. I allowed that guilt and pain to ruin our marriage."

Lesley knew Jordan had been as much at fault as Molly in the breakup of their marriage. Unable to deal with his own grief, he'd buried himself in his work. When they'd become involved, Lesley was well aware that Jeff was the reason Jordan had refused to consider a family. Because she knew how much he'd suffered when he and Molly had lost their son to SIDS, she'd agreed.

"That night in Manuka, I conceived Bethany," Molly admitted sheepishly.

"Thank heaven you did," Lesley said with a light laugh, "otherwise both our lives would have been drastically different." Lesley and Jordan might possibly have married and that would have been a tragic mistake.

"Jordan and I owe a tremendous debt of thanks to Zane."

Zane. He hadn't told her, hadn't so much as whispered a word about his past. He'd been a hired gun. A hired killer.

He hadn't trusted her enough to tell her the truth, and because she was so caught up in preparing for the wedding—the one he insisted take place by the end of the month—she hadn't thought to ask.

His past had seemed irrelevant. She knew he'd traveled extensively, and that the injuries he'd sustained had been the result of some military campaign. She'd assumed—she'd believed—he was retired military. She'd never probed into his life before moving to Sleepy Valley and he'd never volunteered. If he'd held back the truth in this matter, it made her wonder what else he was hiding from her.

"How did Jordan know about Zane?" Lesley asked once her head was clear.

"They're old army buddies."

So she was right about that at least. Zane had been in the military at some point.

"Are you ready for lunch?" Molly asked enthusiastically.

"Sure." It was difficult for Lesley to conceal her feelings. She felt as if she'd been hit below the belt, but she did a good job of keeping up a front while they headed for the restaurant. She needed to talk to Zane, confront him with what she'd learned. But she wouldn't be able to do it before the wedding. Zane was out of town. A business trip, he'd explained.

For the first time since accepting his proposal, she nourished doubts. He'd left town with little more than a message on her answering machine. The trip was unavoidable and he'd be back the night before the wedding.

The wedding. It was going to be a small private affair with only their immediate family members, and a handful of close friends.

Until that moment, Lesley's biggest uncertainty for the outside wedding had been the weather.

She didn't feel she had any choice. She was calling off the whole thing. It would be impossible to enter into this commitment until there was complete and total honesty between them.

When they arrived at the restaurant, Lesley was so caught up in her thoughts that she didn't realize the room was filled with friends and business associates.

"Surprise." The cry went up like a stage curtain and shocked her. Stunned, she looked to Molly for an explanation.

"It's a wedding shower," her friend explained and hugged her close.

A bridal shower for a woman about to cancel the wedding.

Carl had made an excuse every day for two long, torturous weeks to see Candy. He'd taken her to dinner damn near every night. He'd sat through more movies in that period than he'd seen in the past ten years. They'd gone on a picnic. He'd taken her horseback riding. One afternoon, she'd even convinced him to go sailing, and Carl hated the water.

It shocked him to what lengths he'd been willing to stretch in an effort to convince her to let him make love to her.

He'd bought her gifts, too. Why, he'd damn near bought out the chocolate display at Buckwald's. Candy's house was wall-to-wall flowers, and for good measure he'd thrown in a case of wine, a bottle of perfume and some bubble bath.

The bubble bath had come close to ruining him. He groaned aloud every time he thought about Candy bathing, her scrumptious body drenched in nothing but tiny bubbles.

After each and every outing, Carl had come away feeling like he'd slammed his head against a brick wall. The most she'd allowed him was a few token kisses and an occasional taste of her breasts.

Just enough to keep him hooked. Just enough to tantalize him into imagining more. Even now he couldn't believe he'd allowed her to string him along for the amount of time she had.

As of this moment, Carl was through making a first-class fool of himself. As far as he was concerned, he'd proved himself in spades. If Candy thought he would put up with any more of this lolly-gagging around, then he had a thing or two to tell her.

When he phoned to suggest they get together that evening, Carl had made it sound as though nothing had changed. Candy had agreed easily enough, but then, she'd done that almost from the first.

He arrived right on time, only this night he didn't come bearing gifts. She opened the door and smiled sweetly at him. Like she had every day for the past fourteen, she seemed right pleased to see him.

"We need to talk," he said, stepping into her home and plopping himself down on the sofa.

Her eyes widened at his gruff manner. "Is something wrong?"

"Sit down." He pointed toward the chair across from him.

Frankly, it surprised him that she was so willing to do as he asked. The woman had a penchant for making his life miserable, and it wouldn't have surprised him had she stood there and argued.

"We've been seeing each other on a regular basis for two weeks now," he said, keeping his eyes trained on her.

"Yes." Her smile was deceptive, gentle and kind. Carl was convinced she'd taken a great deal of delight in making him suffer.

"Every time I've taken you out, I've brought you a gift, just so you'd know how important you are to me."

"I don't need the gifts, Carl. You've gone overboard on that."

She was telling *him!*

"At the end of the date, you let me kiss you."

She demurely lowered her eyelashes. He nearly laughed aloud. There wasn't a retiring bone in this woman's body.

"I want to know how much longer it's going to take, and I want a straight answer."

She blinked as though she hadn't a clue what he was talking about. "How much longer?"

"Before we make love." He damn near shouted the words. "A man can only take so much frustration, and I have to tell you, I reached my limit a good ten days ago." It was impossible for him to sit still. He sprang to his feet and loomed above her.

"Are you saying the only reason you took me out was because you wanted to get me into bed?"

Carl knew a trap when he saw one. He hadn't spent all that time in the battlefield without gaining a few insights into the way a strategist's mind works.

"Not entirely," he told her. "The fact is I've enjoyed getting to know you." And he had. But not one of the evenings had ended the way he thought they should.

"But making love weighed heavily into your decision to date me?"

He eyed her, wondering where she was leading, fully expecting her to steer him into a bog of verbal quicksand. "Yes. Damn it, Candy, we're good together."

Her eyes lit up as though he'd said the magic words. "I think we're good together, too. These last few weeks have been some of the happiest of my life. Spending time with you, getting to know you and letting you know me has been wonderful."

"Don't you think all this time spent together should lead to a natural conclusion?" His gaze fastened on her bedroom door at the end of the hallway. "Candy," he whispered, "can't you see? I'm half-crazy wanting you." He didn't mention, although she must have noticed, he'd been suffering from perpetual frustration.

Her eyes were tender and Carl was sure she was going to see things his way.

"I agree spending time together does lead to a natural conclusion."

At last. Carl was so damn eager to have her that he pulled his shirt loose of his waistband. "Oh, baby, I didn't know what I was going to do if you refused me." He unsnapped the cuffs of his shirtsleeves and started working the buttons free.

"Carl, that natural conclusion should be marriage, don't you think?"

Marriage!

Carl froze. He felt as if he'd been sucker punched. So that was what she wanted. So that was what all this was about. It amazed him that he hadn't seen through her act earlier.

He pointed his finger at her while he started toward the front door. The jaws of the trap were fully exposed now.

"No way."

"What do you mean, no way?" Candy was back to her normal self. Her hands were planted against her hips and her eyes tossed fire at him a flame thrower couldn't reproduce.

"I'm not the marrying kind." He wouldn't give in on this one, so she'd best get used to the idea right now.

"And I'm not the type to sleep around."

The suggestion angered him beyond reason. "I only want you to sleep with me. You've already done it once, so what's the big deal?"

"You better get something into that thick skull of yours, Carl Saks." She held up her bare left hand. "I am not going to bed with you again until there's a ring around my finger."

He laughed, and not because she was being particularly funny. The woman was a loony tune if she thought she could trick him into marrying her.

He headed for the door. "You might have spelled that out earlier and saved us both a lot of trouble."

Because she had no way of contacting Zane, Lesley was forced to wait until the morning of the wedding. After a sleepless night, she arrived at his home before eight.

From the smells drifting out from the kitchen, it was obvious that Mrs. Applegate had been cooking since the wee hours of the morning. Zane's housekeeper had insisted upon supplying everything for the reception herself, including the wedding cake.

"You aren't due here for hours yet," Mrs. Applegate chided, wearing a wide, happy grin.

"I need to see Zane."

The housekeeper's eyes widened with shock. "You can't do that. Don't you know it's bad luck for the groom to see the bride on the wedding day? One shouldn't take this sort of timeless advice lightly."

"Mrs. Applegate, please, it's important."

The older woman was clearly perplexed. "He isn't here," she announced stiffly in what Lesley was convinced was a lie.

"Then I'll find him myself."

"You can't, dearie, you just can't," Mrs. Applegate insisted, blocking the doorway.

Lesley hadn't thought she'd have trouble getting past the housekeeper. If the situation wasn't so ludicrous, she'd cry.

With little effort, she was able to sidestep the older woman. No sooner had she stepped into the entry hall than Zane appeared at the top of the stairs.

"Lesley." He sounded pleased to see her.

"I tried to stop her," Mrs. Applegate called up to him. "You and I both know it's bad luck to talk to the bride before the wedding."

"Lesley, what's wrong?" His eyes delved into hers as he ignored his housekeeper.

"We need to talk." The sooner she told him of her decision, the sooner they could contact the guests.

"Come into the library." He then directed his attention to Mrs. Applegate. "Could you bring us coffee? It looks like we could both use a cup."

"Of course." The housekeeper returned to the kitchen, looking none-too-pleased with either one.

Lesley walked over to the fireplace and placed her hand against the mantel. Her heart was racing. "You didn't tell me," she said.

"Didn't tell you what?"

"That you were a mercenary."

Her words were met with silence. "We both have our secrets."

"That's not true," she cried.

He arched his brows. "You never mentioned that you were once almost engaged to Jordan Larabee."

Chapter Eight

"That's different," Lesley insisted. "Jordan wasn't in love with me... and I wasn't... didn't think... we never..." She tried to explain, but her tongue kept getting in the way. Abruptly snapping her mouth closed, she glared at him. "How long have you known?"

"Two days." He spoke casually, as though it were of little importance to him. As if she were overreacting to the news he'd been a former mercenary. "It wouldn't have mattered, Lesley. There was no reason to keep it from me."

She felt the heat crawl up her neck. The entire time she'd dated Jordan, Lesley had been uncomfortably aware that he was a married man. While it was true he and Molly were separated, nevertheless, Lesley had been uneasy. Again and again Jordan had assured her there was no chance of a reconciliation between him and Molly. Lesley had wanted to believe that and so she'd overruled her objections.

"We each have a past," Zane reminded her gently. "I'm fairly confident that over the years we've both said and done things we regret. As far as I'm concerned, that's where all this belongs. In the past."

"But..." He made sense and that concerned her. Her fear was that she so badly wanted to marry Zane, she was tempted to overlook everything else. The same way she'd tried to ignore the fact Jordan was still married to Molly while they dated.

"What you learned about me is true," he said evenly. "I was once a paid soldier, but I've made a new life for myself now, here in Sleepy Valley."

With his injuries it would be impossible for him to return to that life-style, she reminded herself. Those days were behind him, and he was looking to her for his future. Just as she counted on him for her own.

"I can't force you to marry me—that decision is yours. But if you want to call off the wedding, then you'll need to make up your mind soon." He glanced at his watch. "By my estimate, our guests will be arriving in less than four hours. What's it to be, Lesley?"

It didn't pass her notice that he didn't offer her any inducements. He didn't attempt to sway her with pretty words. Not once had he claimed to love her. He offered his life without promises, without guarantees. It was a take-it-or-leave-it affair. For all the emotion he revealed, her decision mattered little to him.

"What's it to be?" he repeated.

Zane had always been fair with her. He could have lied any number of times, and hadn't. She respected and admired him for that. As he claimed, the past was over and done. Nothing would change that. So he hadn't lived the life of a saint. Neither had she. Some of her mistakes had been glaring.

He held himself stiffly away from her as he waited for her answer. Lesley raised her head until their eyes met. He held her look for several moments, but she was able to read nothing.

"We're both crazy," she whispered. Enough people had told her that for Lesley to start believing it.

"Agreed," he said smoothly.

She briefly closed her eyes and prayed she was making the right decision. "I think you'll make me a good husband, Zane Ackerman."

For the first time that morning he smiled. "I certainly intend to try."

The wedding took place at noon. Zane stood at Lesley's side at the viewpoint that overlooked Lake Michigan. He felt his grandmother would have approved.

The sun shone gloriously, and the sky was clear blue and bright. A happy omen, he'd like to think, but he wasn't foolish enough to believe there weren't plenty of clouds on the horizon, plenty of storms ahead for Lesley and him.

He had played it cool with her that morning, and his gamble had paid off. He'd gone so far as to tell her that her relationship with Jordan didn't bother him, but even as he said the words, he realized it was a lie.

The little green monster was an alien emotion to Zane. It had taken him the better part of two days to identify the emotion. As soon as he learned that Jordan and Lesley had once been involved, he realized that his longtime friend was the reason Lesley hadn't married.

She'd claimed otherwise, but it didn't add up. When Molly came back into Jordan's life, Lesley nobly stepped aside, but she carried her heart on her sleeve as far as the other man was concerned. It all made a crazy kind of sense.

As he'd claimed earlier, they'd both made their mistakes. He couldn't criticize Lesley for entering into this marriage with her own agenda. He had one, as well.

Zane repeated his vows in a deep, strong voice, harboring no qualms. No second thoughts. No fears. He pledged his heart and his life to her without reservation. When he finished, he discovered her staring up at him and offered her a reassuring smile.

Lesley repeated her own vows in a clear, smooth voice, her gaze held by Zane's.

When Zane slipped the solitary diamond on her finger, his heart swelled with fierce pride. She was his wife now, and there was no turning back for either of them. That was just the way Zane wanted it.

Following the reception, under a barrage of rice and well wishes, Lesley and Zane hurried to his car. He drove them to a secluded cabin deep in the woods for a four-day honeymoon. It was unfortunate, but Lesley couldn't take more time from her work. If she'd had time to properly plan the wedding, she could have asked for vacation time, but Zane had been unwilling to postpone the wedding even one month. She never had understood his rush.

"It's lovely," she said, standing next to her suitcase in the middle of the large open room. The two-story log structure belonged to a friend of Zane's.

Huge picture windows overlooked the meadow below where a field of wildflowers exploded with vivid color. The fireplace dominated another wall, and a thick imitation bearskin rug was spread across the polished hardwood floor.

"Are you hungry?" Zane asked, after delivering their luggage to the bedroom.

Lesley shook her head, although she'd barely eaten all day. All at once, she realized she was nervous.

"It looks like we might be in for a storm," Zane commented, walking over to the window and glancing at the sky.

"A storm?" That seemed impossible when only hours earlier there hadn't been a cloud in sight.

"I'm partial to storms myself," her husband admitted, staring at the darkening sky. His hands were clenched behind his back.

Lesley remained where she was. A number of times she'd considered the physical aspect of their relationship, but with everything so hectic before the wedding, they'd never discussed it. She wished now that they had; it might have helped diminish her nervousness.

"You like the rain?" she asked.

Zane looked over his shoulder, grinning at her sheepishly. "How soon you forget."

Lesley blushed. She had forgotten. The first time he'd kissed her had been the night of the storm when she'd gone out to the barn with him to settle the horses. Later, as the thunder had boomed overhead and the lightning blazed across the heavens, she'd made her way downstairs and found him in the library.

"I wanted to make love to you that night," Zane admitted in words so low, she had to strain to hear him. "I've never stopped wanting you." Slowly he turned to face her.

Lesley moistened her suddenly dry lips.

"I'm not a handsome man."

She wanted to contradict him, but couldn't find the strength to do so. Never had she desired a man as much as she did him right that moment.

"My body is less than perfect." He kept his hands behind his back, and his eyes steadfastly held hers.

Lesley's breathing went shallow, as she started unfastening the buttons to her silk suit. Her movements seemed to mesmerize him into speechlessness. She removed her jacket and blouse, then paused long enough to fold and neatly set them aside.

"Lesley?" Again his voice was a fragile thread of sound.

"I certainly hope you aren't about to suggest we delay making love," she said, and reached behind her to fiddle with the skirt zipper. The zipper rasped open in the tense silence that followed.

Zane didn't answer her question and she glanced up, waiting. He stood frozen in place. It looked almost as if he'd stopped breathing.

Lesley stepped out of her skirt and neatly placed it on the chair with the blouse and jacket. She stood half a room away, wearing her tap pants and bra.

Zane didn't move. Although the room had darkened with the approach of the storm, he couldn't conceal the effect she had on him. She focused her attention on the bulge in his pants and experienced a happy sense of satisfaction.

His arousal fueled her own. Her nipples tightened, beading against the satiny texture of her top. He made no move toward her, but a wild look filled his eyes. His feet were braced apart and his arms remained behind his back. His breathing swelled his chest and he seemed to be taking in deeper and deeper breaths and holding them longer and longer. Although he didn't move, didn't speak, she could feel the tension in his body.

"Do you still want me, Zane?" she asked. The role of the temptress was new to her, but she found she enjoyed it.

His eyes drifted shut, and she didn't know why he was fighting her so hard. His Adam's apple moved up and down in his throat.

Mumbling something she couldn't understand, he started to undress. His hands were quick, the action jerky and disconnected in his rush.

"Yes, I want you." He swore under his breath when he couldn't remove his shirt fast enough to suit him. He wadded it up and carelessly tossed it aside. His stomach was flat, smooth and hard, and while she would have taken pleasure appreciating it more, he squatted down to remove his shoes. He unbuckled his belt next, and slipped his pants over his lean hips, revealing the extent of the injuries to his leg.

The scars that mangled his flesh caused her to draw in a deep breath. How he must have suffered. At her soft gasp, Zane glanced her way but didn't hesitate as he stepped out of his pants.

"I told you what to expect." He offered neither apology or explanation. He glanced toward the loft where the master bedroom was situated and to the stairway leading to it.

"Not there," she whispered.

His questioning eyes returned to her.

"Here." She sat on the rug in front of the fireplace and enjoyed the soft feel of the rug against her skin. It didn't take him long to ease down beside her.

He leaned forward and kissed her with infinite care. The kiss was long and slow and deep. His hands cupped her breasts, gently squeezing and exploring their texture. He broke off the kiss long enough to remove her top and press her down against the thick texture of the rug. As he pressed his rough palm against the smooth skin of her abdomen, he claimed another deep kiss. His hand slipped past the elastic waistband to the silky triangle of curls blow. She was moist and hot and sighed aloud when his finger parted the gentle opening to her femininity.

She panted while he stroked her into a fever pitch and then swallowed her moans with a kiss while she writhed on the verge of ecstasy.

"Zane." She broke off the kiss and tossed her head from side to side. "Please ... I need you so much."

He removed the tap pants and then positioned himself above her, spreading her legs to make room for his hips to fit against her. Closing her eyes, she inhaled sharply as she felt the hard length of him enter her. Hot and swollen, he eased himself inside her until he could go no farther.

Neither moved. Neither breathed.

He braced himself on his forearms and leaned down and kissed her. The kiss started out tender, but as he began to move, the tumult overtook them and the kiss became as fierce and wild as their lovemaking. Zane's tongue sought out hers, dueling and mating in tune to their bodies joining.

Lesley whimpered, and lifted her hips from the rug, meeting each of his thrusts as the fever mounted to unbearable levels. At her peak, her body shuddered and she cried out.

Zane groaned and tossed back his head. He gripped her by the hips, aligning her in an effort to fit more solidly in her. His own completion followed seconds after her own, his powerful body convulsing as he shouted in exultation.

Afterward he held her close, his breathing harsh and heavy. Lesley wrapped her arms around him, buried her face in his neck and silently wept. He'd given her only pleasure, but the beauty of what they'd shared demanded an emotional release, and that came in the form of tears.

"Lesley?" He gently stroked the hair from her face.

She shook her head, not wanting to answer him.

"I hurt you?"

"No . . . no."

He reversed their positions so that she was above him. He continued to smooth her hair as he held her close.

"Will it always be this good?" she whispered when she could.

Zane kissed the top of her head and slowly exhaled a deep breath. "I sincerely hope not."

Confused, Lesley raised her head to look at him and saw that he was smiling.

"A man could die from this much pleasure."

Lesley laughed and closed her eyes. That being the case, they both just might be dead before the end of the week.

* * *

Carl was not a happy man. Zane was married, which was shocking enough, and now Candy was looking to slip a ring through his nose. Well, he had news for her. Zane might have taken leave of his senses, but not so with Carl. He'd as soon leap off a bridge as take a wife.

Every time he thought about how Candy had led him down a merry path, it irked him. He should have known better than to trust a woman. She'd been plotting against him from the first, and he'd damn near fallen for it.

Carl walked into the kitchen and vented his frustration by slamming the door.

"When are Zane and Lesley due back?" he asked Mrs. Applegate.

"Monday," the cook said, ladling soup into a bowl. "Sit down. Lunch is ready."

"What kind of soup is that?"

"Chicken noodle."

He hadn't had much of an appetite lately. "I think I'll skip lunch."

She emptied the bowl back into the pot. "Suit yourself. I don't know what burr's under your saddle, young man, but I suggest you take care of it."

Carl glared at the older woman. Even the kindly housekeeper had been in a surly mood of late. It used to be that they'd laugh and joke.

"You've been snapping everyone's head off for the last week. What's the matter with you?" she demanded. "I swear you'd complain if they hung you with a new rope."

Carl growled a response and slammed the door on his way out, just as he had on his way into the kitchen.

He hated to admit it, but the old woman was right. Damn it all—he was angry. Most of his irritation was directed at Candy, but he wasn't feeling kindly toward Zane, either.

Married. Zane. It didn't add up.

Frankly, Carl was worried, but what Zane did with his life was his own business. Carl knew his friend wouldn't take kindly to any advice or interference.

Carl was willing to admit that his mood had deteriorated in the past week without Candy. He hoped that she missed him enough to come to her senses. In thinking back over their last conversation, he realized that he'd been vague about what he intended to offer her. He'd be a generous lover and it was only fair that she know that.

She'd had a week to realize the error of her ways. He refused to allow a woman to manipulate him and she'd best learn that right now. But on the other hand, it was only fair that he give her an opportunity to apologize.

It felt as though a weight had been lifted from his shoulders as Carl climbed into his truck. He'd bet a year's pay that Candy had been miserable without him. More than likely she'd be grateful he gave her the opportunity to set matters right.

He whistled as he drove into town and parked in front of the feed store. Not wanting to appear obvious, he'd gone to the trouble of making up a list of several items he needed. None of them were essential, but she didn't know that.

Carl spied Candy the minute he walked into the store. Her gaze zeroed in on him, as well. Damn, but she was a sight for sore eyes. Pretty as he remembered. More so, he decided. Generally she wore jeans and a shirt to work—not so this day. She had on a

Western-style blouse and an ankle-length denim skirt with a lace-fringed petticoat that was three or so inches longer than the skirt. Just seeing her again, the ache inside him intensified tenfold.

"Good afternoon, Carl," she said, leaving Slim to deal with the one other customer in the store.

He was right, she'd missed him! To show her what a forgiving kind of guy he was, he returned her smile full measure. His heart gave a happy lurch.

"What can I do for you?"

He'd almost forgotten about his list. He reached inside his shirt pocket and handed it to her.

She took it and briefly scanned the contents. "You picked up worming medication the last time you were in. Are you sure you need it again?"

"Throw it in anyway." He knew what he did and didn't have in stock.

"This doesn't look like it'll be a problem. Do you want me to have it delivered?"

If he did, there was a chance she'd send someone out with it and not come herself. "I can take it with me now."

"Sure thing." With the piece of paper in hand, Candy paraded around the store, collecting items.

Carl followed her. "How have you been?" he asked conversationally. He tucked his thumb inside his belt loop and struck a casual pose. He didn't think she would be honest enough to admit she'd been lonely without him, but it would be a nice touch if she had.

"Good," she answered absently, gathering together his goods and stacking them on the counter. "How about yourself?"

"Fine, just fine." He tried to make it sound as though he hadn't a care in the world. "I decided to buy the Gaudette spread. I put earnest money down on it Wednesday."

"Congratulations." She glanced his way and smiled approvingly. She did seem genuinely pleased. Many an afternoon had been spent with her, reviewing his ideas for the property. He was taking her advice on a number of items.

"It looks like the deal will close within six weeks." He felt good about having made that decision. "I thought you'd want to know that I've decided not to cut down those apple trees." He'd made the concession because she felt so strongly about those trees. One of them needed to extend an olive branch first.

"That's great. If you want a recommendation for someone to prune them, let me know. Hank Harris over at the nursery does an excellent job with that sort of thing."

"I appreciate knowing that."

She tallied his order and he paid her. There didn't seem to be much more to say. "See you later."

"Have a good day."

"You, too." Carl headed toward the door, then hesitated. He wasn't ready to leave yet. He hadn't told her any of the things he'd wanted to say. It was a shame to come all the way into town for a load of supplies he didn't need.

With a bag tucked under his arm, he followed Candy to the back of the store. She was three rungs up a ladder, shuffling salt blocks from one shelf to another. The sight of her derriere thrust at eye level tantalized him to the point of distraction and he found it necessary to look away.

"I'd like to talk to you," he suggested, making sure his voice contained just the right amount of friendliness, but not overly much.

"Anytime," she said, twisting around and glancing down at him.

"How about a cup of coffee?"

"When?"

When the hell did she think? "Now suits me."

"Sorry, Carl, I can't. Eric Kitsap is stopping by."

"The veterinarian?"

"We're driving into Chicago this afternoon."

"What for?" he demanded. What Carl knew about Eric Kitsap he didn't like. Mainly that he was a young buck who looked as if he had plenty of wild oats yet to sow. Carl wanted it understood, right now, that he wasn't about to let Candy anywhere within a hundred feet of the new veterinarian.

She glared down at him. "That's none of your business, Carl Saks."

"I'm making it my business."

She sighed heavily. "As it happens, we're attending a dinner."

"Over my dead body." He clenched his teeth, ready to do battle right then and there if necessary.

The friendliness had left Candy's eyes, replaced by a chill that would have caused a lesser man's blood to run cold.

Then it dawned on him that he was doing it again, playing right into her hands. Candy had set him up on purpose, just to make him jealous. He nearly fell for it. The woman was crafty—he'd say that for her. Well, he wasn't any dummy. He'd let her stew in her own juices.

"You're absolutely right," he said, backing away. "It isn't any of my business. You could date a different man every night of the week if you wanted."

Candy moved down two rungs on the ladder so that they were eye level. It demanded every ounce of self-control Carl possessed not to bring her into his arms. His knees felt weak for need of her.

"Is that what you want, Carl?" The question was so softly asked that for a moment he thought he imagined it. "Do you want me dating other men?"

She was about to set him in another trap. He couldn't very well confess that it did plague him for her to see another man. Nor could he lie and not have her know it was a bold-faced fabrication.

She stared at him intently, awaiting his reply.

He frowned, and then growled out the truth. "It bothers the hell out of me, but if the price of having you exclusively means a ring through my nose, then I say you can date every man in town, because I'm not willing to sacrifice my freedom for you or any other woman."

He thought he saw tears mist her eyes, but then was sure he was mistaken. The woman was nothing if not proud.

"That answers that," she said and turned away from him.

With nothing more to say, Carl wandered outside. He didn't experience a sense of triumph the way he should. Instead, the loneliness he'd experienced in the past week seemed to yawn even wider.

Lesley hummed softly to herself as she washed the few dishes they'd dirtied over breakfast. Soon they would head back to Sleepy Valley, and the following day she was scheduled to return to the office.

Her time with Zane had been idyllic and she hated it to end. These few days in the cabin would be all the honeymoon they would have.

Between the renovation project, Mrs. Applegate and Carl, the house would hum with activity. Her own work schedule was hectic. It was unlikely Lesley would be able to share much uninterrupted time with Zane again for a number of weeks. Especially since she would be making the ninety-minute drive to and from the office every day.

Zane moved behind her and slipped his arms around her waist. He turned her in his arms for a slow, warm kiss. After the past few days and nights of lovemaking, they were familiar with each other's bodies. There was no reason to be reticent, no reason for either of them to be shy.

"The car's packed."

"I'll be finished here in a few minutes." Pressing her head to his shoulder, she whispered, "I don't want to go back, Zane. I want to stay here forever with you."

He didn't answer her with words. Instead, he located the opening to her blouse, slipped his hand inside and cupped her breast. The small intimacy caused her to shiver. With her back against the kitchen counter, Zane quickly unfastened her blouse. She moaned when his lips closed over her nipple and she arched against him. When she discovered he was already aroused, it seemed poetic justice to stroke her hand down the front of his jeans. Soon Zane groaned.

Lesley offered no resistance when he carried her to the rug that had initiated their lovemaking on their wedding night. He unsnapped her jeans and shoved them down to her knees.

She had trouble unlatching his belt buckle.

''Hurry,'' he said urgently, as though he couldn't wait a moment longer.

The minute she released the zipper, he shifted her back, mounted her and guided himself into her warm, moist center. They both groaned together as her inner muscles stretched to accommodate the full length of him.

Lesley had lost count of the number of times they'd made love in the past few days. In no way did his injuries impede his lovemaking.

She knew he wanted a child—they'd discussed that frequently—but he seemed to be on a mission to accomplish the deed in record time.

Zane began to move and she accepted each mighty thrust until a harsh groan tore from his throat and his powerful body was racked with shudders. Her own completion followed almost immediately.

Zane buried his face in her neck as he struggled to bring his breathing under control. Closing her eyes, she savored the moments together.

In the silence that followed, he held her close. It didn't trouble her that he'd never told her he loved her. The words weren't important; he proved it in other ways. She was aware that once their physical hunger had been sated, they would need to learn to communicate on other levels, but for now this was enough.

During the three-hour drive back to Sleepy Valley, Lesley propped her head against Zane's shoulder. Neither spoke much. Zane seemed as aware as she about what changes their life would take upon their return.

Mrs. Applegate was on the porch to greet them when Zane pulled into the driveway. The housekeeper threw open her arms as though they'd been away for years instead of a few days.

"Welcome home," she called out, then rushed down the stairs and hugged Lesley.

"Thank you. It's good to be home."

Zane tucked his arm around Lesley's waist. "How's everything been here?"

"Good. No trouble."

"Great." Together they walked into the house. Zane moved to the library and started sorting through the mail.

"I've got a special dinner all planned for you two this evening." Mrs. Applegate clenched her hands together as she described in details each course, starting with wild rice mushroom soup.

"It isn't necessary to go to all that trouble, Mrs. Applegate," Lesley admonished. She should have known better.

The woman looked offended. "Of course it is. By the way, your things arrived and I took the liberty of unpacking them in the master bedroom."

"Thank you." Lesley's eyes followed Zane. He was poring over a letter and frowning heavily.

"Bad news?" she asked, joining her husband.

He didn't answer.

"Zane?"

He looked at her as though she hadn't spoken. "Is there a problem?" she queried.

He attempted to reassure her with a weak smile. It didn't work. Whatever was in that letter had deeply distressed him. It troubled her that he wasn't comfortable enough with her yet to share whatever it was.

Mrs. Applegate outdid herself with dinner, and Lesley raved over the prime rib, but it didn't escape the cook's notice that neither Lesley nor Zane appeared to have much of an appetite.

Following dinner, Zane returned to the library. Lesley followed and closed the doors.

"You might as well tell me, you know."

His eyes rounded with surprise. "Tell you what?"

"Something is obviously wrong. I noticed it when we first arrived home. As soon as you read that letter." She motioned toward his desk.

His response wasn't really an answer. "I have to go away for a few days."

He didn't offer any reasons, didn't volunteer any other details.

"When?" she asked.

"I don't know—soon."

"How soon? Next week, next month...?" she persisted.

He didn't answer.

"How long will you be away?"

He hesitated. "A week, maybe longer." Again he offered no additional information.

She knew that he wasn't any keener on going than she was on having him leave. But drilling him with questions he didn't want to answer would serve no useful purpose.

"I'll miss you," she said softly.

The intensity with which his eyes darkened told her that he felt the same way.

Chapter Nine

The pain in Zane's leg intensified as he continued with the physical therapy. He'd been working out three and four hours each day in an effort to build up his endurance. His routine rarely changed. He started with straight leg lifts, then leg curls, followed by hip adductions and toe and calf raises.

Sweat broke out across his forehead as he gritted his teeth and focused his concentration on working his injured thigh, hoping to regain what mobility he could.

The feeling of urgency drove him to push himself harder and harder. He had to leave Lesley soon. Very soon. Had to find Schuyler before the temptation to stay grew too strong to resist.

In retrospect, Zane realized he'd been incredibly naive to think he could marry Lesley and not fall in love with her. When he'd learned about her relationship with Jordan Larabee, his feelings had been mixed. He strongly suspected she held some tenderness for the contractor. Being the noble, kind person that she was, Lesley had stepped aside in order to give Jordan and Molly the opportunity to give their marriage a second chance.

A part of Zane had been relieved to know about Lesley's involvement with Jordan. If she continued to love Jordan then she wasn't as likely to care as deeply for him. After Zane was killed, she'd mourn his death, but it wouldn't devastate her, and that comforted him.

At the same time, Zane had nearly been consumed with jealousy. The thought of Lesley loving another man ate at him like a school of piranha. Again and again he forced himself to remember that they'd both gone into this marriage for specific reasons, none of which had to do with love.

Now, without warning, the rules had changed. For the first time in his life, Zane Ackerman was falling in love.

Attaching any romantic sentiment to their marriage was something he'd never intended. It was both foolish and dangerous to become emotionally involved with Lesley, and yet it seemed impossible not to love her.

In the weeks since their wedding, Zane had grown accustomed to having his wife at his side. When she left for the office in the morning, he counted the hours until her return.

Each night he anxiously anticipated her homecoming. By four o'clock he actively watched the time, wanting to be there to personally welcome her home. He worried about the long commute, feared an accident, but said nothing.

Following dinner, they often sat in the library and talked over a cup of coffee. Zane had come to appreciate her wit and her intelligence. More and more he realized how fortunate his child would be to have Lesley for his or her mother.

Following their wedding, his nights, once filled with demons and nightmares, became Zane's favorite part of the day. A thousand times he reminded himself he wasn't a teenager and that his fierce physical need for her was sure to burn itself out soon. He was wrong. His physical desire for her hadn't waned.

Zane tried to convince himself that the sole purpose in their lovemaking was to impregnate Lesley quickly. Once the deed was done, he would be free to go after Schuyler the way he'd vowed. Once he was certain Lesley carried his child, there would be no excuse to linger. At the rate with which he worked to that end, he didn't think it would take more than a month or two. He actively prayed it wouldn't.

For the first time in his life, Zane felt completely and utterly content. It took him far longer than it should have to acknowledge he was happy, although it seemed to be obvious to everyone else. Even Mrs. Applegate took delight in telling him so.

"I thought I'd find you in here." Carl Saks strolled into the exercise room and broke into his thoughts. Carl hesitated before he asked, "Have you got a minute?"

Zane was grateful for an excuse to quit his exercising, and reached for a hand towel. "Sure." He wiped the sweat off his face. "What's on your mind?"

Carl was looking almost haggard these days. They rarely talked, and since the wedding, his friend had taken to eating his meals alone. Zane knew it wasn't anything personal. Carl was offering Zane this time to be with Lesley, and if he guessed right, Carl had his own love interest.

"The bank phoned this morning and everything's progressing smoothly with me buying the Gaudette property. It looks like I'll be moving at the end of the week."

"That soon?" Zane didn't realize he'd spoken aloud until Carl responded.

"Actually, I'm grateful to have a place of my own."

Zane could well appreciate that, but he felt fortunate that Carl had stayed on this long. "It's not going to be the same around here without you," he said.

"You've got Lesley now," Carl said.

A smile gladdened Zane's heart at the thought of his wife. She'd be home soon, and he'd be leaving. Damn, but he was going to miss her. In two days time he'd be leaving for a week. Zane dreaded going, hated the thought of seven torturous days and nights without her. But it was necessary if he was going to find Schuyler. The news he'd received gave him cause for concern. There was a possibility the terrorist had discovered Zane was alive.

"Married life seems to agree with you," Carl said. He walked over to the minirefrigerator and helped himself to a cold beer. Zane opted for a soda.

Zane shrugged, not sure how to answer his friend. His marriage wasn't a comfortable subject for Zane. "How are things going between you and—" He wasn't allowed to finish the question.

"They're not," Carl snapped. "She refused to sleep with me unless there was a ring around her finger." He took a quick, deep swallow of beer. "The woman's unreasonable, and as far as I'm concerned, I'm better off without her.''

Zane had difficulty hiding a smile. "So she wants you to marry her."

"Have you ever heard anything so ridiculous in your life?''

Zane laughed outright. "I can't say that I have."

The sarcasm flew over Carl's head. His friend seemed to forget that Zane was a newlywed himself.

"She's been dating the new vet in town," his friend continued, and his jaw tensed. "Apparently she's hoping it'll make me jealous. It isn't going to work, but she doesn't know that. I refuse to allow a woman to manipulate me. I told her up front that I'm not the marrying kind, and she best accept it right now 'cause I'm not changing my mind."

Carl's face was flushed with anger by the time he finished.

Zane held up both hands. "Peace. Peace."

"Sorry. I guess my feelings are more heated than I realized." Then all at once Carl seemed to understand what he'd implied. "I'm real glad for you and Lesley, though," he added quickly. "Frankly, I never thought I'd see the day that any woman could maneuver you to the altar. I guess it took someone like Lesley." He hesitated. "Don't get me wrong. I couldn't be more pleased for you. Lesley's a hell of a woman."

Zane didn't want to talk about his marriage. "Thanks," he said shortly.

"I've got to tell you I was getting downright worried about you going after Schuyler," Carl went on to say, more relaxed now. "It's a suicide mission and we both know it."

Zane turned his back on his friend, unwilling to discuss his plans with Carl. He should have realized it wouldn't be easy to fool his friend.

"You have abandoned the idea, haven't you?"

It took Zane a long time to answer.

"Haven't you?" Carl stressed.

Zane could see no way to avoid the truth. "No."

The silence between them felt loud enough to break through the sound barrier.

"What do you mean—no?"

"I made a vow." Carl of all people should appreciate the seriousness of his words. Dan and Dave had been brutally murdered by a madman. Zane had stood over their grave sites and vowed revenge.

Carl's gaze narrowed slightly. "If you intend to find Schuyler..."

"I do." Zane wanted no room for misunderstanding.

"Then, do you mind telling me what possessed you to marry Lesley?"

The question was hurled at him, a mixture of disbelief and anger. Carl's gaze bore holes straight thought him.

"What's between Lesley and me is my business."

"Does she know what you're planning?"

"That's none of your affair."

Carl tossed the half-empty beer into the waste can. "I can't believe this." He plowed his fingers through his hair. "This is crazy." He straddled the bench, and glared at Zane. "There comes a time in life when a man faces a bridge."

"You're beginning to sound like Mrs. Applegate," Zane said, striving to look bored.

"Either you cross that bridge, or you burn it."

"At the risk of repeating myself, let me remind you that what I do with my life is my business."

Carl stood abruptly and studied Zane intently. "Lesley doesn't know, does she? Of course she doesn't," he said, answering his own question. "You married her without her knowing you fully intend to get yourself killed."

"Keep Lesley out of this." Zane was fast losing his patience. He stood and clenched his fists at his sides. "I know what I'm doing."

"You're sacrificing your life."

"I'm avenging Dan and Dave. They were like family to me, and I will not let their murders go unanswered."

The two men scowled at one another.

"Zane." Lesley's sweet voice drifted from the hallway. She came into the exercise room. Zane tore his gaze away from Carl to greet his wife. Her happiness bubbled over as she hurried into his arms. Zane briefly held her against him and closed his eyes. Her smile was potent enough to brighten the darkest corners of his heart.

"I hope I'm not interrupting you?" Lesley glanced apologetically to Carl.

"Are you going to tell her?" Carl demanded, ignoring her question. "She has a right to know."

Clearly confused by the aggression in Carl's voice, Lesley hesitated. "Tell me what?"

Candy carried a load of groceries into the house and set the two bulky sacks on the kitchen counter. She'd purposely chosen to shop at a store where she wasn't as well-known. The last thing she needed was for some clerk to announce to everyone in Sleepy Valley that she'd bought a home pregnancy test.

Candy didn't know what to think. Generally she was regular as clockwork, but this time she was late. Later than she'd ever been. Closing her eyes, she flattened her hand over her stomach. A knot formed in her throat at the prospect of being pregnant.

It would be just like Carl to think she'd done this on purpose, as if he weren't a contributing factor. She hadn't talked to him in twelve days. It was the longest stretch of time they'd been apart since...since that fateful afternoon. He was ignoring her, or pretending to, but Candy knew otherwise.

Apparently, Carl didn't understand what living in a small town meant. Every time he asked about her, the news made its way back to her. From all she was hearing, he was doing a lot of asking.

Mostly, his inquiries had to do with her seeing Dr. Kitsap. If the man had any brains in his head, he'd realize Eric Kitsap was a kid fresh out of veterinarian school.

It was true they'd gone to dinner a couple of times, but it was nothing serious, nor was it likely to develop into anything more than friendship.

Candy emptied the groceries onto the counter, then neatly tucked them inside her cupboards. The pregnancy test glared at her with accusing eyes until she finally took it into the bathroom and set it on the back of the toilet. She'd confront that issue later, when she'd built up her nerve.

She could be carrying Carl's baby.

There was no need to worry about that now, she told herself, putting on a brave front. If she *was* pregnant, she'd deal with the matter the way she had with everything else in her life—straight on with no excuses.

In an effort to put some order to her troubled thoughts, Candy walked out front and reached for the green garden hose. Her rose bushes were beginning to look peaked. She often watered her flower beds when she needed to think matters through.

Because she was so caught up in her thoughts, she didn't hear Carl until he spoke.

"Candy."

She whirled around, shocked to find him standing on the sidewalk on the other side of her white picket fence. The first thing she noticed was how pale he looked, as though all the fight had gone out of him. She couldn't—wouldn't—agree to his terms, but she hadn't the energy to fight him.

"Hello, Carl."

"I was in the neighborhood and thought I'd stop by."

If ever she heard a lie, it was now, but she didn't call him on it. Antagonizing him now would serve no useful purpose.

"Can I come in?" he asked, his eyes dark and serious.

She nodded, still too shocked to respond verbally. The garden hose continued to spew out water as she stood there transfixed by the man who'd occupied her thoughts day and night for weeks on end.

"You could invite me inside."

"Of course…" Forgetting the hose was in her hand, she gestured toward the house and thoroughly doused the front of his shirt and pants.

Carl swore and leapt back.

Candy looked at him in shocked horror, then burst out laughing.

"This isn't funny," he growled, slapping his hand against his front in an effort to get rid of the excess moisture.

Candy hastily turned off the water and moved inside the house to provide him with a towel. She hadn't wet him on purpose, but she couldn't think of anyone who deserved it more.

"Take off your shirt and I'll stick it in the dryer."

He stripped it off and handed it to her. She realized her mistake the moment she saw how broad and muscular his shoulders were. His powerful chest was marked by a patchwork display of short curly hair.

They'd made love, may have even created a child together, but this was the first time she'd ever seen Carl without his shirt. The sight was something to behold.

Unfortunately, letting him know that would be a mistake. "It might be best if you kept your pants on," she mumbled, and made her way to the laundry room.

"I disagree," he said.

She was surprised to realize he'd followed her. Standing there next to the dryer, she dragged a deep breath though her lungs. Leave it to Carl to turn the tables on her. Generally, her wicked tongue got her out of embarrassing situations like this one, but she felt completely devoid of wit. Her heart hammered wildly, and she feared she would blurt out something stupid and he'd immediately guess she might be pregnant.

"What?" he asked her softly. "No witty reply."

He was behind her, so close, she could feel his breath stir the soft hairs at the base of her neck.

"I...I..."

He braced his hands against the smooth skin of her shoulders. His touch was light and gentle. So very gentle. Shivers of awareness chased up her arms.

"You've missed me, haven't you, baby?"

Candy closed her eyes and bit her lower lip. The ability to lie effectively had long since deserted her. She had missed him. Dreadfully so.

He eased himself against her, tucking his front securely against the rounded curve of her buttocks. His voice was seductive and low as he slipped his hands from her arms and around her front to capture her breasts. To her dismay, her nipples immediately puckered as if to issue their own silent encouragement. When he used his thumbs to rasp against their beaded hardness, Candy was obliged to swallow an involuntary moan.

"I've missed you," he whispered before he lowered his mouth to her neck. His tongue made moist circular movements against the highly sensitized area while his hands worked their magic on her breasts.

He had her jeans unsnapped and had worked open the zipper before she realized what he was doing. Even then, she hadn't the strength to resist him. He dragged the lower half of her body back, tucking her more intimately against his tortured sex. All the while, his tongue licked at her senses, firing them to life. Whispering how much he needed her, he caught her earlobe between his teeth and sucked gently.

Candy drew in a shaky breath when he eased his hand past the elastic of her waistband and flattened it against the smooth skin of her abdomen. His breath rasped against her neck as he stretched toward the delicate array of soft feminine curls. Involuntarily, Candy parted her thighs.

"That's it, baby," he whispered huskily. "Open for me."

It was as though his voice came from a great distance. She had no resistance left in her. None. She squeezed her eyes closed and rolled back her head as he inserted his finger deep inside her liquid heat. She arched and stifled a sob as he began to stroke her, igniting every nerve ending with fire. Within seconds, under his manipulations, she felt her body soaring toward relief.

"No," she gasped, as the rippling shudders began to claim her. "No..."

"Yes, baby, yes." Carl's rasped voice sounded in her ear as her body convulsed against him. "That's it," he whispered gently. "That's it. Good, baby, good."

Her breathing sputtered and her heart felt as though it were about to explode. This couldn't be happening. Not here. Not in her laundry room with a man who only wanted one thing from her. Not with Carl who promised her nothing, and demanded her soul.

When she was convinced he had wrought every ounce of pleasure from her that her body was capable of supplying, he freed his hand and twisted her around.

With a sob, Candy buried her face in his shoulder, embarrassed beyond belief, mortified to the very marrow of her bones. With a few delicate strokes, he had managed to make her body sing for him in three-part harmony.

Carl cupped her buttocks and crushed her against the throbbing protrusion in the front of his pants. "I need you, Candy."

Not giving her time to think, he claimed her mouth in a bone-melting kiss. Their tongues mated in a frenzy of need.

"Let me show you how much I've missed you," he managed between kisses, his lips tugging at hers.

It cost her the earth to break away from him.

His eyes revealed his shock.

Candy wiped the hair away from her face. She was confident her cheeks were candy apple red. "I can't."

He groaned and closed his eyes. "We've been all through that. I'll be good to you, baby."

"Good? Define good. You'll seduce me in the laundry room? Is that good?"

He looked bewildered and confused. "I never intended for this to happen. It just did, but it was great. It's always great with us. You can't deny that."

He was right—she didn't have a leg to stand on.

"I want you to move in with me," he ordered, leaving no room for argument. "I'm moving into the Gaudette place this weekend. We've talked about it so often, it's only right that you be there with me." He reached for her hand and kissed her knuckles. "The house needs a woman's touch... Hell, forget the house! I need you."

He was offering her a place in his life, which was something she'd never thought he'd do. It was a step, but not in the right direction.

"I've never asked a woman to move in with me. I want you to know that." He wrapped her in his arms. "If you don't want that, then fine. But, baby, I've got to have you. You're driving me crazy. I don't sleep nights. I've lost my appetite. If it bothers you that people will talk... well, we can be discreet. Only, I can't play these games any longer... It's bad for us both."

Candy braced her forehead against his shoulder. "What... what if I were to... you know... get pregnant? Would you be willing to marry me then?"

He broke away from her so abruptly, she nearly collapsed.

"Pregnant?" He said the word and gave a short laugh. "No way. Okay, okay, you want to talk about kids. Fine, we can do that, but not for a long time."

"How long?"

"Years. Just don't make the mistake of thinking you can convince me to marry you because you're pregnant. That might work with another man, but not me."

All at once, Candy was so furious that it was impossible to see beyond the red haze of her anger. "You're an idiot." Her rage made the words nearly unintelligible. "Do you think I got pregnant on purpose?" she shouted. "It takes two, you know."

He glared at her as if she were speaking in another language.

"Get out of my house."

"You're pregnant?"

She shoved his shoulders, steering him toward the front door.

Carl's mouth hung halfway to his knees. "Are you telling me you're already pregnant?"

"Get out before I phone the police, and don't think I won't, Carl Saks. Don't make the mistake of believing I wouldn't derive a great deal of pleasure throwing your sorry butt in jail."

The front door was open and she gave him one last shove. His shoulders hit the screen door with enough force for him to wince.

She started to close the door, and would have taken a good deal of pleasure in slamming it in his face. But at the last moment, he moved.

The door shut with enough force to rattle the windows.

Candy leaned against the wood frame and wrapped her arms around herself. The only person who could reduce her to this was Carl Saks. The sooner he was completely out of her life, the better.

"I wish I knew what it was you and Carl argued about," Lesley told her husband. They sat in the study, drinking coffee. Lesley noticed that Zane seemed less communicative this evening. She suspected it had something to do with the confrontation with his friend.

"Zane?" she probed when he didn't immediately respond.

"That's between me and Carl."

Lesley felt a tightness take hold of her chest at his words. Zane shared so little of himself with her.

"I heard Carl tell Mrs. Applegate he's moving this weekend."

Again Zane acted as though he hadn't heard her speak.

"I hope it's not because of your argument."

"It isn't."

Lesley couldn't stand it. She tossed the newspaper aside and leapt to her feet. "Stop it, Zane."

He blinked up at her. "Stop what?"

"Freezing me out of your life." She stood directly in front of him, her hands braced against her hips. "I won't stand for it."

"Good." He leaned forward and caught her by the hips. Before she could stop him, he managed to send her tumbling into his lap. She didn't resist, but worried that her weight was too much for his leg. He gave no indication that she hurt him.

His eyes were level with her own and she saw the laughter drain out of them.

"I mean it, Zane." She tried to make her words stern, but by the time they left her lips, they were soft and malleable. Against her will, her anger crumbled into a lazy grin as her husband brought her mouth to his.

"You're so damned beautiful," Zane whispered. He wove his fingers into her hair, wadding the thickness into his fists. "So incredibly beautiful." He sealed his words with another deep, soul-reaching kiss.

"Why is it," she asked, her breath low and wispy, "that you can make me want you this quickly? I should be furious with you."

"Don't be," he pleaded. He made love to her with his kiss, using the movements of his tongue to demonstrate what they would be doing shortly.

"You never told me . . ."

"That I could make you want me?" he teased, unfastening several buttons of her blouse. He folded back the warm blue silk to expose bare skin. His gaze feasted on her breasts as he moved his index finger over the peak and watched as her nipple hardened and puckered.

Lesley had trouble keeping her mind on track. "Carl seemed to think you needed to tell me something."

"It's not important." He pressed his moist mouth over her hardened nipple and sucked gently, wetting the lacy front of her bra.

"Zane..." She came halfway off his lap. "Two can play that game, buster." She hadn't made love with him this often not to know what pleasured him most. He tried unsuccessfully to stop her from reaching for his zipper. Their laughter and giggling nearly prevented them from hearing the knock against the door. "Who is it?" Zane called.

Lesley tried to fasten her buttons, but Zane wouldn't let her.

"Mrs. Applegate. I'm sorry to disrupt you, but Mr. Larabee's on the phone. He wants to talk to Mrs. Ackerman."

"Jordan, oh, my. I forgot...I was supposed to call him after dinner." She hurried off Zane's lap and rushed toward the phone. "I'll take the call in here. Thank you, Mrs. Applegate." She was forever grateful the housekeeper hadn't opened the library door.

Lesley had righted her clothes by the time she reached the phone. She took a couple of seconds to compose herself before she reached for the receiver. "Hello, Jordan."

He'd called for additional information on an estimate he was preparing. As the conversation progressed, Lesley watched as Zane impatiently stood and walked over to the fireplace. His back was to her for several moments. When he turned, she didn't recognize his expression.

There was a time when he'd been able to hide his feelings from her, but she knew him too well now. She'd seen him in pain, and anger. She'd seen him laugh and smile. She'd seen his face in ecstasy when she had the presence of mind herself to study him as they made love. In the weeks since their marriage, she'd witnessed everything in between, but not this. His eyes had narrowed, his nostrils flared slightly and he looked to be waging war with himself.

As best she could, Lesley cut the conversation short and replaced the telephone receiver.

"Zane," she asked softly, "what is it?"

"What's what?" The look was gone; his eyes revealed a detached, dispassionate expression.

"Just now while I was on the phone with Jordan..." She paused, unable to explain with words what she'd seen in him.

"It's nothing," he snapped.

But it was and they both knew it. He walked over to the desk and she placed her hand on his arm. He stared pointedly at her fingers as if he wanted nothing to do with her touch.

Unbelievably hurt, Lesley slowly removed her hand.

"Tell me something," he said in a tight whisper. "Do you still love him?"

Him? This made no sense to Lesley. "Jordan?"

"Of course I mean Jordan. You were almost engaged to marry him, or have you conveniently forgotten?"

The question took her by such surprise that Lesley didn't immediately answer. A cold feeling invaded her heart, extending out in ripples until it reached the very tips of her toes.

"You think I'm in love with Jordan Larabee?" She didn't honestly expect him to answer. The very ridiculousness of the question was lost on him.

"Yes," he responded tautly.

"I see." She wrapped her arms around her middle and stiffened. With a dignity she wasn't feeling, she straightened her shoulders and headed toward the library door.

"Answer me," he demanded. "You're the one who's so fond of asking questions, aren't you? Not more than five minutes ago it was of utmost importance to know the reason Carl and I had argued."

She paused, facing the door. After a prolonged moment she turned around. "Do you honestly believe I'm the type of woman who would allow another man to make love to me night after night if I cared for someone else?"

Zane opened his mouth, but said nothing.

"Only a fool wouldn't recognize how much I love you, Zane." Having said that, she opened the door and walked out.

Two hours later, Zane wandered outside, breathing in the fresh night air in an effort to clear his thoughts. He owed Lesley an apology. He'd behaved like a jealous idiot and she had every right to be angry with him.

He strolled to the viewpoint and was surprised to discover he wasn't alone. Carl sat on the concrete bench, staring into space. Zane sat at the opposite end.

Neither seemed inclined to speak.

"If I asked you to, would you shoot me?" Carl asked.

"Shoot you?"

"At this point it would be a kindness."

His friend was talking in riddles. "Is there a moral to this story?" Zane asked.

Carl wiped his hand down his face. "I keep telling myself this is a nightmare and I'll wake up and it'll all be over."

"What's wrong?"

"Nothing that a good horsewhipping wouldn't cure."

Zane braced his elbows against his knees. "I'm feeling much the same way. I just made a colossal ass of myself."

"You, too?" Carl muttered.

"It must be something in the air." Zane leaned back. "Is there any particular reason you're looking to stand before a firing squad?"

"Yeah. I'm seriously thinking I'm going to marry that little she-devil."

Chapter Ten

The atmosphere at the breakfast table the following morning was decidedly cool. Eyeing Lesley wearily, Zane pulled out the chair across from his wife and poured himself a cup of coffee.

Lesley ignored him. He would have willingly apologized the night before if she'd been awake. But by the time he'd climbed into bed, his wife was curled up in a tight ball on her side of the mattress, fast asleep. Or so she wanted him to believe. Zane knew otherwise, but in this instance the old adage about letting sleeping dogs lie seemed appropriate.

Zane reached for a piece of toast and evenly spread Mrs. Applegate's strawberry preserves over the surface. "It looks like there's going to be another wedding soon," he announced to no one in particular.

Mrs. Applegate delivered a plate of scrambled eggs to Zane.

"Carl and Candy?" Lesley asked. Those were her first words to him all morning.

Zane nodded.

Mrs. Applegate smiled broadly. "I was wondering about those two. I imagine marriage will greatly improve that man's disposition."

Zane didn't mention that Carl seemed downright miserable at the prospect of becoming a husband.

His housekeeper chuckled softly and murmured, "You know, the first baby can come anytime, but the rest take nine months." Having said that, she returned to the kitchen, the door swinging in her wake.

Lesley's gaze found his. "What did she mean by that?"

Zane shrugged. He'd given up trying to decipher his housekeeper a long time ago.

"Could Candy be pregnant?"

"I doubt it," Zane said automatically. Carl wasn't foolish enough to get physically involved with a woman without using protection. But on second thought it made a crazy kind of sense. Carl had mumbled something about shooting himself for being so stupid.

"Maybe she is." He revised his earlier statement. Laughter tickled Zane's throat. He had a difficult time picturing Carl as a doting father, but guessed that once his friend became accustomed to the idea, he'd like it just fine.

Zane searched his wife's face. She looked pale and drawn and he acknowledged that his jealousy had hurt her. He silently cursed himself for behaving like an idiot. He wasn't a man accustomed to apologizing. Even though he recognized he'd been in the wrong, the words didn't come easy.

"About what I said last night..." he muttered, prepared to eat dirt if necessary in order to repair the damage. "I was wrong."

Lesley seemed to find it important all at once to smooth the linen napkin in her lap. When she did glance up, he noticed the pain in her eyes. His insides twisted with regret.

"Is that an apology?" she asked.

He didn't hesitate. "Yes. I realize now that you'd never have married me if you loved Jordan Larabee. I don't make any excuses for the question. Plain and simple, I was jealous."

"And..." she prompted.

"And?" He frowned, not understanding what she wanted from him. Whatever it was, he'd say it, do it, buy it, but he had to know what *it* was.

Lesley scooted back her chair. "I have to be in the office early this morning." Zane was well aware she was using that as an excuse to leave him and avoid his question.

She stood, put down her napkin and walked out of the dining room.

Stunned, Zane sat at the table, wondering what he'd done wrong now. He'd never been good at dealing with women, and he seemed at an even greater loss when said woman was his wife.

Tossing his napkin aside, he stood and followed her. "Lesley," he shouted, stopping her at the front door. "Damn it, what did I do now?"

She shook her head, as if she didn't know herself. "Nothing," she whispered with such misery that Zane felt his heart twist.

"Tell me what it is you want from me," he ordered. "Just tell me." Heaven knew he'd walk over

hot coals if she asked, if that was what she wanted
from him.

"I... thought—hoped—you had something you
wanted to say to me," she whispered miserably.

"Like?"

She shook her head. "If I have to ask you, then it
means nothing."

It dawned on him then. She was looking for him to
say he loved her. Heaven knew he did, although this
was something of a disaster, in light of what he
planned. The words burned his lips, but he found it
impossible to speak.

She recovered quickly, and offered him a weak
smile. "I'm sorry," she mumbled. "I don't know
what's wrong with me. You apologized... That's
enough."

Candy pregnant.

Carl didn't know how many times he'd repeated
those words. Each and every time, no matter how often he said them, an electric shock bolted through him.

He hadn't slept a wink. How like a woman to deliver the most devastating news of a man's life and
then toss him onto the street. Carl had been too
stunned to ask a single question, and before he could
react, he had found himself standing bare chested on
her front porch, dusting off his Stetson. It was a good
thing he'd moved when he did. Another second or two
and her front door would have rebroken his nose.

Damn, but she had a temper. If ever he'd seen a
woman who needed taming, it was Candy Hoffman.
Carl sincerely doubted there was a man in town capable of handling that little hellion. He was probably
the only male in a three-county area up to the task.

She'd given him an ultimatum. Marriage. The word alone was enough to make him cringe. Well, he'd played her little game to the end. With anyone else, it would have been over the minute she'd hinted at a wedding.

He didn't mean to boast but he figured he could have any woman he wanted. That was the problem. He only wanted Candy. Every other female he knew paled in comparison.

She had her faults, that was for damn sure. Never in all his days had he met a more unreasonable cuss. She had a temper that went off like a firecracker. She was stubborn and irrational, and that didn't even begin to describe her.

But then she had her good points, and he wasn't talking about her physical attributes, either. Candy had one of the quickest minds he'd ever seen. She was both intelligent and knowledgeable, and that was only the tip of the iceberg. Sexually he'd never had a woman satisfy him the way Candy had. The one and only time they'd made love had been a frenzy of need on both their parts. Sweet heaven, they hadn't even made it to a bedroom.

Talk about a responsive woman. It turned him on just remembering the scene in her laundry room. If their lovemaking was this good in his living room and her laundry room, Carl could only imagine what it'd be like in a bed.

But marriage?

That seemed like a drastic price to pay for the pleasure of bedding a woman. But if that woman was Candy, it just might be worth it.

Now it seemed, on top of everything else, Candy was pregnant. Despite the shock, Carl found himself smiling. He'd had her only the one time. He wondered what the odds were of impregnating a woman after one time, and knew they were too high for him to calculate. Although he'd be the first to admit it was crazy, Carl felt a certain amount of pride in the fact she was carrying his baby. The two of them were good together. Damn good. A man wasn't likely to stumble upon that kind of chemistry again. Candy could well be woman enough to keep him satisfied the rest of his life.

It went without saying that he'd prefer forgoing the marriage business. But if that was the price he was required to pay, then he'd best do it. It didn't seem that his squawking was going to change her mind.

Carl experienced a small sense of pride in the fact Candy wasn't selling herself short. She'd set down her price and hadn't wavered. He hadn't liked it, wasn't sure he did even now that he'd decided to accept her terms, but he was agreeable.

He rode into town and bought a diamond ring before noon. He tucked it inside his jeans pocket, then stopped off for lunch at the local café.

Never having proposed before, Carl wasn't quite sure how to go about it. One thing was certain, if she expected him to get down on one knee and make a fool of himself by speaking all those fancy words, then she could forget it. He wanted her to know that he wouldn't do this for any other woman. That should be good enough.

A part of Carl hoped Candy would be out making deliveries when he stopped off at the feed store. It wasn't until he parked outside that he was willing to admit he was nervous about all this.

Slim glanced up when he walked into the store. "Candy's in her office," the other man told him.

Carl nodded, obliged at not having to make an excuse to linger until Candy showed.

He found her sitting at a big rolltop desk that had been her grandfather's. She held a calculator, using the eraser end of a pencil to punch in the numbers.

Carl walked inside the compact office and closed the door.

Candy glanced up and wasn't able to disguise the surprise that rounded her eyes. She sighed heavily as if burdened with the mere thought of having to deal with him.

"What do you want now?" she demanded.

"Is that any way to welcome me?" he asked, grinning broadly as he took a seat. He wasn't fooled by her bravado. She was downright pleased to see him and he knew it.

"You're about as welcome as a rattlesnake."

He couldn't help it; he laughed outright at that. One thing was certain—Candy was going to give him a run for his money. The way he figured, they'd move out to the ranch that weekend and be married the next.

"You have something on your mind, or did you come just to make my life miserable?" The words were issued in her usual waspish tone.

"Where's a laundry room when I need one?" Carl muttered under his breath.

"What did you say?"

"I said," he repeated loudly, "what we need is another laundry room."

Apparently this wasn't what she wanted to hear. Candy shot to her feet and clenched her fists into tight

balls at her sides. "How dare you mention that unfortunate incident to me."

"Unfortunate incident," he repeated, doing a
commendable job of holding in his amusement. The
little hellion would take delight in scratching out his
eyes, and he wasn't about to offer her any further incentive.

"I think it would be best for us both if you kindly
left." She sat back down, her chest heaving. She returned to the calculator, posting a long series of numbers.

Although Carl wasn't normally a patient man, he
figured he had nothing to lose by staying right where
he was. When he didn't immediately obey her wishes,
she forcefully expelled her breath.

"We don't have anything more to say to each
other," Candy insisted.

"On the contrary. One doesn't make the kind of
announcement you made to me and leave it at that."

Her cheeks reddened at the mention of her pregnancy. "Don't worry about it, Carl."

"Hey, weren't you the one who so sweetly reminded me that it takes two? I can't help but worry.
That's my loaf of bread you're baking in your oven."

Candy tossed the pencil onto the desktop and stood
up, slowly shaking her head. "My, oh my, you do have
an eloquent way of phrasing things."

"It kinda makes one wonder, doesn't it?" he said,
leaning back in his chair and locking his fingers behind his head, striking a cocky pose. The more he
thought about Candy being pregnant, the more smug
he felt. Not that he was particularly interested in raising a passel of kids. The knowledge that he was so
potent that all it took was one turn at the wheel didn't

hurt his ego any. After they were married, they were going to have to be careful, otherwise they might well be major contributors to the problem of overpopulation.

"Wonder about what?" Candy asked.

"I told you we were dynamite together, didn't I?"

"I told you not to worry about what I told you yesterday. It was a mistake."

She closed her eyes as though struggling within herself. Her chest heaved, calling attention to one of her finest assets. Her breasts. Damn, but this woman had incredible breasts. She did everything humanly possible to minimize them, but Carl knew their beauty. He had held them in his hands, tasted them on his lips. She was a fine specimen of womanhood, but she needed him to help her come to a deeper understanding of how beautiful she was.

Standing abruptly, he walked over to the office door and lowered the shade.

Candy gave him a look of horror and came out from behind the desk. "Just exactly what do you think you're doing?"

He grinned broadly. "Saving us both a lot of embarrassment."

She blinked as though she didn't understand him. "If you so much as lay one finger on me, Carl Saks, I swear I'll scream the place down."

She would, too. Carl knew better than to doubt her, but he also knew that, given the right incentive, she'd be a willing participant in what he had planned.

"I've been doing a lot of thinking about what's happening between us," he said, ignoring her threat.

"Nothing's happening," she denied heatedly.

He gave her a look that said he was disappointed in her lack of honesty.

"All right," she amended quickly. "Nothing's happening from this point forward. I made a mistake...I'm entitled. Everyone's allowed an error in judgment now and again."

"Sure," he agreed readily enough as he slowly made his way toward her. She was backed against the desk, her rear butting up to the flat surface. Her breasts swelled with each breath as he neared.

An elongated moment passed before his mouth claimed hers. She could have stopped him at any point. Could have broken away or pushed him aside. Carl took pride in the fact she didn't.

The kiss was deep, long and near desperate. Her tongue met his, touching, stroking, exchanging as one mind-bending kiss led to another. Carl couldn't get enough of her and the feeling seemed to be mutual.

His hands were on her beautiful breasts and hers were in his hair. It didn't take long for their kisses to become more turbulent and their caresses more and more urgent. It soon became obvious that a little petting and kissing weren't enough to satisfy either of them.

When he was desperate to breathe, Carl dragged his mouth from hers. "Candy."

She squirmed against him, torturing him in ways only she could do. "Yes?"

The momentous moment had arrived. It was now or never. She was warm and pliable in his arms. His hands were on her breasts, she was firecracker hot for him. The odds of her accepting his proposal weren't going to get any better than this.

"There's a ring in my pocket." It wasn't an eloquent proposal, but she should get the message.

Candy went stock-still. Carl noticed that he had her attention now. Even her breasts perked up at his words.

"A ring," she repeated.

He nuzzled her neck with his nose, loving the smell and feel of her. It would take two lifetimes to properly love this woman.

"A wedding ring, darlin'."

He figured she'd burst into tears of happiness or react in some such womanly way. What he didn't expect was for her to jerk herself free and glare at him as if he'd insulted her.

"Why?" she demanded.

"Why? You're gonna have a baby, aren't you?"

She whirled around so fast that papers scattered from atop the desk. When she spoke, her voice was soft and low. He barely recognized it as hers. "Is the baby the only reason you want to marry me, Carl?"

"Yes. Of course." He wasn't going to lie about it. He probably would have reached the same conclusion in time, but the fact Candy was pregnant was a large part of the reason he'd decided they should be married now.

"I see."

Carl frowned, not understanding. "Well," he said, losing patience, "do you want the damned ring or not?"

She turned around to face him then. Her eyes were blank as if she were looking straight through him. "I..."

She was going to reject his proposal. Carl recognized the look in her eyes. By God, after making a fuss

big enough to call in the United Nations to settle, she
was going to refuse him.

He removed his hat and slapped it against his thigh.
"You know, Candy, I'm sick and tired of getting
kicked in the teeth every time I try to do the right thing
by you. You don't want to get married, then fine. I
told you before I wasn't the marrying kind."

She lowered herself to the chair and brushed the hair
from her face. He noticed her hands were shaking.

"I've offered you everything I'm going to. If you
don't want it, all the better. It's time I started searching greener pastures." He started out the door, and
then because it would have been too much of an embarrassment to return the diamond to the jeweler, he
took it out of his pocket. It was a pretty thing, and had
cost him plenty. He tossed it on the desktop. "Take the
ring back if you want. I sure as hell don't want it."

Having said that, he walked out. He was finished
with Candy Hoffman. As far as he was concerned, he
never wanted to see her again.

This time he meant it.

The alarm sounded and Lesley groaned in protest.
She was exhausted. Zane scooted toward the irritat-
ing buzzer and flipped the switch, then cuddled her.
Neither moved, content to be in each other's arms.
Slowly he parted her pajama top and found her breast.

Lesley's soft sigh was filled with appreciation until
she remembered that this was the day Zane was leaving. Within a matter of hours he'd be on a plane. He'd
told her so little about this trip, only that he'd be away
for a week. She didn't even know where he was going,
although she knew he needed his passport.

Carl and Zane had argued again. Whether Carl's move or the disagreement had anything to do with Zane's trip, she didn't know. Zane was keeping something from her. Something vital.

"I have to go soon," Zane whispered.

Lesley rolled onto her back. Zane had propped himself up on one elbow and was gazing down on her.

"I know." Her heart ached, hearing the words.

"I'll be back in a week," he promised hoarsely. She snuggled in the warm shelter of his arms. He held her for so long, she feared he'd miss his flight. Then he kissed her tenderly, slipped out of bed and was gone.

The first day following his departure was the longest. Lesley ate dinner alone and then wandered outside, drawn to the viewpoint she loved so well. This was the very spot where they'd stood only weeks earlier and exchanged their vows.

Her misery had more to do with the secrets Zane refused to tell her. She felt at a loss as to how to read Zane. Although he'd never spoken the words, she knew he loved her. Her distress wasn't entirely emotional. From the moment Zane had left, her body had ached with symptoms that resembled the flu. She couldn't get enough sleep and yet no matter how many hours she spent in bed, she didn't feel rested.

Mrs. Applegate noticed on the third day Zane was gone. "My goodness, look at you. I swear you're as pale as mashed potatoes."

Lesley managed a smile.

"What can I bring you for breakfast?"

Lesley shook her head. She had no appetite. "Not a thing. I think I'll just have coffee and be on my way."

"I won't hear of it. Mr. Zane personally asked me to look after you. Now, I want you to make an appointment with your doctor and I want you to do it today."

Lesley agreed with a nod, simply because it was less trouble to give in than to argue. By the time she arrived at her Chicago office, she felt even worse. The glass of orange juice Mrs. Applegate insisted she drink hadn't sat well.

Her secretary, Alice Unger, followed her to her desk. "Are you feeling all right, Lesley?"

"I don't know. My stomach seems to be a little queasy this morning. Would you see if you could get me an appointment with Dr. Wilson this afternoon?"

"Sure thing."

A half hour later, her secretary informed her that there was an opening with the physician for three that same afternoon.

"I just don't know what's wrong with me," she mumbled when Alice delivered a fax later that morning.

At three-fifteen that same afternoon, Dr. Wilson told her. "You're pregnant."

"Pregnant," she repeated as if the prospect were highly unlikely.

"You were recently married."

"Yes, but..."

"As I recall, you didn't want any form of birth control."

How a highly intelligent woman could overlook what must have been obvious was beyond Lesley. "I'm pregnant," she repeated, her happiness spilling over. "You're certain, aren't you? There's no mistake?"

"Not according to these results."

She hugged the physician and laughed, her joy bubbling inside her.

"I take it you're pleased with the news."

"Ecstatic." The only damper was that she'd have to wait to tell Zane.

Lesley drove home, singing to herself. She walked in the door, wearing a silly, happy smile and, found Mrs. Applegate dusting.

The housekeeper looked up, wearing a worried frown. "Did you see the doctor the way I asked?"

"I did indeed," Lesley said, hugging the older woman as she waltzed up the stairs.

"And?" The housekeeper braced her fist against her hip and stared at Lesley, silently demanding an explanation.

Lesley paused halfway up the staircase. "Zane and I are going to have a baby."

"A baby?" The housekeeper, who'd been so astute about Carl and Candy, looked shocked with the news. "A baby," she repeated. "Why, that's wonderful news. I know Mr. Zane is going to be as pleased as punch."

"I think he will be, too."

"A baby is just what this house needs."

Lesley couldn't agree with her more.

That night, as she readied for bed, Lesley stood naked in front of the full-length mirror. She was going to have a baby. She pressed her palm against her flat stomach and sighed with a happiness too deep to express with words.

A new life grew within her. She closed her eyes, remembering the times they'd made love since their wedding night. Zane's beautiful kisses, the tender way in which his body had filled hers, had loved her. Together they'd created this new life.

How Lesley longed to share the news with Zane. He hadn't phoned, not once. Each night she sat by the telephone, waiting, hoping to hear from him, but to no avail.

The day he was due back, Lesley didn't drive into the office. She wanted to be there when he arrived home, wanted to rush down the stairs to greet him, wanted to throw herself into his arms, kiss him senseless and tell him about the baby.

The picture in her mind became reality early that afternoon. The instant she heard the airport limo, she flew down the stairs and outside. Zane had no sooner climbed out of the car when she shot down the porch steps and into his arms.

Her husband caught her by the waist and whirled her around.

Their kisses were frenzied and urgent.

"I take it this means you missed me," he said, laughing.

"Yes. Oh, Zane, I have wonderful news."

"Give me a chance to catch my breath, then we can sit down and talk." He tucked his arm around her shoulder and led her toward the house.

"Welcome home, Mr. Zane," Mrs. Applegate greeted. Her eyes met Lesley's, eager to know if she'd told him about the baby yet.

"It's good to be home," Zane said. If he noticed the silent signals between the two women, he didn't comment.

"Not yet." Lesley mouthed the words and the housekeeper nodded.

"You make yourself comfortable and I'll bring you both in a spot of tea."

"Excellent idea," Zane said, taking Lesley's hand and leading her into the library. "What are you doing home this time of day?"

"I couldn't bear driving into the office. Not when I knew you'd be here."

The moment they were alone, Zane hauled her into his arms and kissed her with a hunger that was close to brutal. With a low, guttural moan, his tongue probed deep inside her mouth. "I thought I'd go crazy without you," he whispered, and eased his good leg between hers. They kissed again, but were interrupted by Mrs. Applegate clearing her throat.

"There's a nice man here who needs to know where you'd like these items taken."

Zane propped his forehead against Lesley. "Have him bring them in here," he instructed.

Lesley buried her face in his neck, but laughed as she overheard Mrs. Applegate explain to the limo driver that they were newlyweds.

Zane reached inside his jacket pocket. "I picked this up in a little jewelry shop in Paris. I hope you like it."

Lesley's gaze widened at the size of the emerald-and-diamond ring. "Zane," she breathed softly. "It's beautiful."

"Try it on and see if it fits."

The ring was only the beginning of the things he'd bought her. There was a necklace to match the ring, a solid gold pen and lingerie that made her blush when she unwrapped it.

He brought chocolates for Mrs. Applegate and seemed embarrassed when the housekeeper got teary-eyed.

"I have something for you, as well," Lesley told him.

"You said you had good news."

"Sit down," she said, directing him toward his favorite chair, next to the fireplace. When he was comfortably seated, she eased herself onto his lap. He leaned forward and kissed her with enough hunger and passion that she nearly forgot everything else.

"I had one hell of a time buying you that lingerie," he whispered. "I'd imagine what you'd look like with it on and . . . shall we say, a certain part of my anatomy found the image much too tempting to ignore."

"Zane," she admonished. "I'm trying to tell you something important."

"Sorry. It's just that it's so damn good to see you."

"I was sick while you were away."

The laughter drained out of his eyes. "Sick. Did you see a doctor?"

"Yes, right away."

"And?"

This was the moment she'd been waiting for. "And," she said, struggling to hold her happiness inside her just a moment longer, "he told me the most incredible news. Oh, Zane, we're going to have a baby."

"A baby," he repeated slowly.

He sounded as shocked as she'd been when Dr. Wilson had delivered the news.

"Isn't it wonderful."

"A baby," he repeated. "That's wonderful, Lesley."

She gave him an odd look. She would have staked her life that he'd be as thrilled as she was, but from the indescribable pain that came into his eyes, one would think this was the worst thing that could have happened to them.

Chapter Eleven

Long before Zane accepted a mission, he carefully calculated each aspect of the operation. He studied every minute detail, every potential for disaster. He accepted full responsibility for his men, drilled them on technique, and was known to be a stickler for detail.

With a history of such caution, it shocked him that he married Lesley with so little forethought. He'd gone into the marriage with his head in the clouds. He'd assumed he could live with her, make love to her and, when the time came, walk away from her and feel nothing.

In light of what he'd discovered in Paris, learning she was pregnant was a blessing. He had to leave her. God help him, he didn't want to go, but he had no more excuses. To linger might put Lesley in danger. No longer could he rationalize staying with her.

In the past, dying hadn't worried him. He'd flirted with danger all of his life, challenged the odds, stared death and deception in the face without a trace of reluctance.

It wasn't dying that plagued him now, it was leaving Lesley and their child. He had to do it soon, otherwise he doubted that he could dredge up the courage to go. Courage. A trait he'd possessed in abundance until he met a warmhearted architect who loved him enough to look beyond his scars, beyond his faults, and selflessly offer him her love.

Zane experienced a deep, spiraling pain. He'd failed Lesley in so many ways. He had to tell her, had to give her an explanation, but he hadn't considered that until she'd told him about the baby. He rubbed a hand down his face and leaned back in the leather chair as he contemplated the unpleasantness of the task. She deserved to know that when he left, it was highly unlikely he'd return.

Moonlight softly illuminated the library, casting golden shadows against the book-lined walls. Sleep had escaped him from the moment Lesley had joyously announced her news.

Zane realized his reaction had puzzled her. She'd thought he'd be happy, and he was, more than she'd ever realize. But the pregnancy was his signal. Mission accomplished.

"Zane." His wife's soft voice interrupted his troubled thoughts.

Zane glanced her way guiltily. "What are you doing up?" he asked.

"I was going to ask you the same thing. This is the third night in a row you haven't been able to sleep. Is something wrong?"

"Not a thing," he promised.

"I can't help thinking—" she paused and yawned loudly, placing her hand in front of her mouth "—there's something wrong."

"There's nothing for you to worry about."

She yawned again. She needed her sleep, more now than ever. A fierce protectiveness stole over him. "You should be in bed."

"I don't sleep well when you're not there."

Soon he'd be gone forever, he reminded himself. She'd best adapt now. He stood to escort her up the stairs so he could return to his solitude. He wrapped his arm around her waist and she leaned her head against his shoulder.

"I'd like to ask something of you," Zane whispered, pressing his head to hers. The thought of her driving into the city every day had plagued him from the beginning. "Now that you're pregnant, could you work from home?"

"Here?"

"I know your job is important to you, and that you're a vital part of the firm, but I've never been comfortable with you making the long drive into Chicago every day."

"Others do it," she protested.

"But no one else is pregnant with my child."

She smiled softly at that. "I'll need an office here at the house."

"Make whatever arrangements you need."

"I'll still probably have to drive in a couple of times a week."

"Fine, just as long as it isn't every day." They entered the bedroom and Zane pulled back the covers for her. When she stared up at him with round, pleading eyes, he knew he couldn't walk away. A few minutes, he told himself, just a few minutes, and climbed in beside her.

As if by instinct, she snuggled into his arms, her head on his shoulder. "Are you sure you're happy about the baby?" she asked in a voice that was barely audible, almost as though she were afraid of the answer.

"Very sure." He pressed his palm against her bare abdomen. He meant it as a gesture of reassurance to prove the sincerity of his words. The backlash of sudden emotion ambushed him. His child grew inside his wife.

His child.

Zane had never been comfortable with emotion. For a good portion of his life he'd eliminated anything that had to do with feelings. Buried them. Ignored them. Denied them.

He'd gone into this marriage discounting any possible sentiment he might attach to Lesley or their child. He'd completely discredited the possibility of falling in love. Now he was left to face the overwhelming consequences.

He wished he knew the baby's sex. He knew Lesley would delight in calling him a chauvinist if he confessed to wanting a son. At the same time he realized that it would probably be easier for her to raise a daughter since she would be alone. Of course, there was always the chance Lesley would remarry.

The shaft of sudden pain at the thought of another man taking his place in her life and bed, raising his child, was almost more than Zane could tolerate. His breathing shallowed as he struggled with the monumental task of contemplating this possibility.

"Is it your leg?" Lesley whispered, reaching toward his thigh. She mistook his emotional agony for physical.

He didn't answer and allowed her to massage the muscles of his upper leg. Her stroking fingers had an instant and curious effect upon him. He swallowed, slowed his breath and grabbed hold of her wrist.

"Enough," he told her between clenched teeth. It was agony sleeping at her side night after night, wanting her with a desperation that rocked him. He was afraid. A man who looked death in the eye feared a slip of a woman, feared his hunger for her would injure their child. He worried that loving her would forever mark his soul.

He felt her smile as she relaxed against him. "We won't hurt the baby, you know."

Zane gritted his teeth. Not with pain, but with the physical struggle necessary to resist her.

"We haven't made love since before you went away," she reminded him, gliding her hand toward the swollen evidence of his need. This time, Zane hadn't the strength to refuse her. When her nimble fingers closed around him, he gasped. His breath hissed between clenched teeth.

He wanted to be gentle when he kissed her, but the ability was beyond him. His lips were hard and demanding, and her passion matched his. His tongue forged her lips and she took it, twining her own tongue with his.

Gradually the kiss gentled as he plowed his fingers through her hair, loving the taste of her, exulting in the generous way she responded to him.

"You're sure I won't hurt the baby?" He needed reassurance as he gathered her body beneath his.

"Positive," she whispered with a small, glad laugh. "Besides, it will please her mother a great deal."

"Her?" he chided.

"All right . . . him."

He kissed her again with an urgency that left him weak.

"Zane, oh, Zane, what took you so long? I've missed you so much."

Two days and it felt like an eternity. His body was ready to explode and they'd only just begun. Feverishly he trailed kisses down her throat, blazing a trail to her breasts. She moaned and arched upward when his lips closed around the hardened nipple. Her fingers dug into his hair, her words incomprehensible as he suckled.

They made love intensely, and cried out in unison at their mutual release. Zane couldn't believe he'd waited this long, when he'd needed her this badly. Never again.

For a long time afterward he held her. She fell asleep in his arms, her bare legs entwined with his. Again and again his hand stroked her hair as he contemplated the future and the monumental task of telling his wife he was leaving her and their unborn child.

Lesley had known something was wrong with Zane when they'd arrived home from their short honeymoon. A mysterious letter had awaited her husband, and from that moment forward, everything had changed.

Whatever was troubling Zane seemed to be linked to his secretive trip. Since his return, he'd been withdrawn and edgy. Depressed and miserable. He wasn't sleeping well, either. Lesley had hoped he'd voluntarily tell her whatever the problem was, but thus far he'd been tight-lipped and uncommunicative. She wanted him to trust her.

His unexpected reaction to the news of her pregnancy continued to trouble her. She assumed he'd be as pleased as she was, but after she'd made the announcement, he'd barely said a word. He'd always been gentle with her, and was still. His thoughtful looks were often tender, but she had the distinct feeling he was emotionally detaching himself from her. Emotionally erecting a wall between them. Each day, it was an effort to scale the fortress guarding his heart.

Lesley needed to know what was happening. One thing was certain—she wasn't going to hear it from Zane.

Carrying a glass of ice tea with her, she walked out to the viewpoint and sat gazing at the white-capped swells on Lake Michigan. Zane was gone for the afternoon. She hadn't a clue where. All he'd told her was that he'd be away for most of the day.

Hearing footsteps behind her, she glanced over her shoulder to find Carl. Zane's friend had moved into his own house a week earlier.

"Is Zane around?" Carl asked.

"He's gone.... I don't know when to tell you he'll be back."

Carl nodded and would have left if she hadn't spoken again, surprising herself with the abruptness of the question. "Why's he doing this?"

Carl slowly shook his head as though he, too, couldn't understand. When he spoke, his words were heated with frustration and anger. "It's insane, I tell you."

Lesley didn't know what had caused her to blurt out the question, but now that she had, she waited, wondering if she should continue this game of words. Carl seemed to think she knew something, when she didn't.

"Did he tell you when he's going?" Carl probed her for information.

"No." Lesley closed her eyes. Zane was leaving again? He hadn't said a word to her, hadn't so much as hinted.

"Soon, I imagine," Carl mumbled. "I'm sorry, Lesley. Nothing I've said changed his mind." This last part was filled with a baffled kind of anger.

"It's insane." She repeated what he'd said earlier, hoping that would encourage the other man to supply the details.

"More than that. It's suicide."

Lesley caught her breath. "Suicide?"

"Zane's no match for Schuyler, not physically. Not anymore. Now that Schuyler knows he's alive and coming, Zane's lost his one advantage. Don't think Schuyler isn't lying in wait for him. The son of a bitch will take a good deal of pleasure in finishing the job. He's going to kill Zane the same way he killed Dan and Dave."

The glass of ice tea slipped from her numb fingers and toppled onto the thick grass. The breath seemed frozen in her lungs.

"Why is he going?" From some hidden resource she found the serenity to keep her voice calm and even as she bent to retrieve the glass.

"The hell if I know. I thought he'd come to his senses when he married you." Carl paced the area in front of her, his short steps revealing his agitation. "I've tried to talk some sense into him. I tried to reason with him, but he made a vow and he won't go back on that—not for anything."

"What about his vow to me?"

Carl hesitated and looked to her. The intensity of his gaze wavered before he glanced away. "He loves you. He never counted on that...but then, I made the same mistake with Candy." The first part of his words were brusque, the latter filled with an indescribable thread of pain.

Lesley placed her hand protectively against her stomach. "I'm pregnant."

Carl looked stricken. "You, too?"

"Too?"

He removed his hat and splayed his fingers through his hair. "Never mind."

"What about the baby? What about me?" she asked, unable to disguise the swelling panic. Zane was going to leave her.... A suicide mission?

"I can't answer that," Carl told her wearily, and she felt his frustration as keenly as her own. "He's going after Schuyler and worse, Zane fully intends to die."

"No," she cried, unable to stop herself. She rushed toward the house, fury and panic fueling her steps as she raced across the yard.

Lesley barreled into the kitchen and Mrs. Applegate whirled around. "My heavens, child, what's wrong?"

"Where's Zane? I need to talk to Zane."

"He's gone, remember?" The housekeeper's words were gentle, concerned.

Lesley knew her eyes were wild as she grabbed hold of Mrs. Applegate's shoulders. "Where is he? I need him. I have to talk to him...have to convince him to stay."

"Come sit down," the older woman said in soothing tones, and led Lesley into the library. "Sit down and relax, otherwise you'll hurt the baby. I'll get Mr. Zane for you, now don't you fret. He'll be home in a jiffy. I'll bring you in a pot of tea and everything will be fine in a few moments."

Lesley was convinced that nothing would ever be fine again. She was sobbing uncontrollably now, her shoulders rocking back and forth in an effort to put some measure of order to her thoughts. Nothing made sense. Nothing added up.

Zane had married her, given her his child and now he intended to leave her for a suicide mission. He intended to leave her, to go off somewhere and die.

She didn't know how long she sat there staring into space, fighting a pain so deep, she couldn't think, couldn't move, couldn't feel. A shocking numbness attacked her senses.

"Thank heavens you're home. It's Lesley. Something's terribly wrong." Lesley heard Mrs. Applegate's voice but it seemed to come from a great distance through the fog of pain.

"What happened?"

Could that urgent voice belong to Zane?

"I don't know. She came flying into the kitchen, screaming for you."

"The baby? Is something wrong with the baby?" Again this was from Zane, and panic echoed with each word.

"No, no," the housekeeper assured him. "She was crying out for you."

Lesley remained frozen, unable to move. The mahogany doors glided open and Zane entered the library.

"Lesley?" He said her name softly and knelt down in front of her.

Her hands were tightly clasped together and she kept her head lowered, refusing to make eye contact.

"What's upset you so much?"

The searing pain in her heart felt as though she'd been branded with a white-hot iron. Slowly, pride and anger dictating her actions, she lifted her head. Her eyes clashed against his. Fury and outrage bounced against gentle concern.

"Who's Schuyler?" she demanded in words as cold as an Arctic wind.

Zane stiffened. "Who told you?"

"Who's Schuyler?" she asked again, louder.

Her husband stood, his movement awkward because of his leg.

"I have a right to know."

"Yes," he agreed readily enough. "Every right." He sat down on the ottoman and leaned forward, pressing his elbows against his knees. He didn't speak and Lesley was fast losing patience.

"What about the letter?"

"It was from a friend. He told me he suspected Schuyler knew I'd survived the explosion. I had to find out if that was true, because it took away any options I had. Now that he knows I'm alive, there's no guarantee he won't come after me. I can't risk putting you and the baby in jeopardy."

"You can't fight. Not any longer...not with your injuries."

"Perhaps, but don't be so quick to think I want to die. I've never had more of a reason to live. Please understand, I wouldn't leave you if it wasn't necessary."

"Can't you hire someone else?"

"No," he answered emphatically. "I refuse to bring anyone else into this. What happened is between Schuyler and me. I already carry the guilt for the loss of two good men, more family to me than any I'd had until meeting you. I won't take on the responsibility for more blood spilled."

"Dan and David?"

He seemed surprised that she knew their names. "Yes." He reached for her clenched fist, swallowing her hands with his own. "They were like brothers to me. We'd been together nearly twenty years." His eyes hardened. "Schuyler murdered them in cold blood right before my eyes. He thought he'd killed me, too, and he damn near had." His fingers tentatively went to his face, touching the reddened scar. "I wanted to remember what he'd done to my friends. That's the reason I never bothered with any cosmetic surgery."

"What about Carl? Can't he help you…can't he go with you now?" she cried, taking another tactic.

"I go alone."

Lesley hung her head, unable to assimilate all that he was telling her. She couldn't get past the feeling that she'd already lost him. It struck her then that she'd never really had him to lose.

"Schuyler is a terrorist, Lesley. He preys on the innocent, takes delight in murder. He often works alone, and that makes him all the more difficult to locate, but word came yesterday that he was hiding in Egypt. I'm going after him now. That's where I was earlier, making my travel arrangements."

"No," she cried, and because she couldn't bear to let him go, she threw her arms around his neck and clung.

Zane's hold on her was tight, his breathing shallow. "I never meant to love you."

The words were bittersweet. "Why'd you marry me? Why?"

He hesitated.

"By your own words, you never intended to fall in love with me."

"I wanted a child."

Too stunned to speak, Lesley closed her eyes in an effort to take it all in. "A baby?"

He didn't respond. It took her far longer than it should have to realize what he was saying. He believed he was about to die and it was important that he have an heir. She was little more than the means to the end. This was what he'd meant when he claimed he'd never meant to love her.

"You used me." Outrage and fury demanded that she stand, although she wasn't sure her weak knees would keep her upright. "You wanted a child and I was little more than a womb... a means of achieving an end. Why the hell didn't you donate to a sperm bank?"

"Please, Lesley, listen."

"I've heard all I care to." She stormed out of the library, climbed the stairs and collapsed on their bed.

Zane gave her a few minutes and then followed. He stood in the doorway to their bedroom. "I don't blame you for being angry. You deserve a far better husband than I'd ever be."

Although she knew it was childish, she covered her head with a pillow and refused to listen.

"I don't have time to pander to your anger," he said harshly. "If you hate me, all the better."

She slowly sat upright and glared at him. "I despise you."

He didn't flinch. "I don't blame you. But listen, there are some things you need to know. You have the rest of your life to hate me."

He entered the bedroom, then stopped abruptly. "I went to see an attorney this afternoon."

"An attorney?"

"Everything I have is yours and the baby's."

"I don't want anything of yours," she spat out.

"Fine. Leave it for the child."

Lesley closed her eyes. He was going to do it. He was actually going to leave her.

"I stopped off and talked to Carl. He's promised to do whatever he can to help you and the baby. He might be a bit rough around the edges, but he's a good man. I wouldn't trust you and the baby's care to anyone else."

"No!" she cried in protest, but Zane ignored her.

"One last thing."

Not only was Zane leaving her, but he seemed determined to go right that minute. "You have every right to hate me. I hate myself for involving you in this craziness. You *do* deserve a husband who's a hell of a lot better than I'd ever be."

She wanted to plead with him to stay, but knew it would make no difference. She stiffened her shoulders and glared at him, refusing to give him permission to hurt her further.

"After the baby's born," he said in a voice she barely recognized as his own, "tell him or her... tell the baby how much I loved their mother."

Even now he hadn't the courage to say it to her face. Hadn't the nerve to look her in the eye and tell her he cared, as if doing so would weaken him.

"Is that all you have to say?" she asked coldly.

"Yes." He started to turn away and she climbed off the mattress.

"I'd like to add one thing."

Zane turned back. She walked over and stood directly in front of him, her chest heaving. Her eyes filled with tears as she struggled to hold in the emotion. His features blurred until he was unrecognizable.

Then, with all the strength she possessed, she raised her hand and slapped him across the face.

The pain in his chest felt like a tight knot. Zane loaded his gear into the back of the pickup and resisted the urge to glance toward the house. It wasn't the way he wanted to tell Lesley goodbye, but perhaps this was best after all. It would be easier to adjust to his death if she hated him, and God knew he'd given her enough reason to do exactly that.

He'd made few tactical errors in life as big as this one. Only a selfish bastard would abuse Lesley. She offered him paradise and in return he was giving her hell.

He recalled when he first introduced the subject of marriage, how he'd mentioned that their union would be monetarily beneficial to her. Lesley had thrown the mention of money back in his face, yet it was all he had to leave her. That and her hate.

Regrets multiplied a hundredfold. He'd been unfair and cruel to the one person who meant the most to him. All he could do was pray that someday she'd find it in her heart to forgive him.

When he couldn't bear to not look any longer, he glanced toward the house. Toward Lesley. Toward the child he would never know.

Pain clenched at his heart with regret so deep, he couldn't breathe. He was leaving behind everything he would ever love. That had been Lesley's greatest gift to him.

Love.

He'd found it in her arms. And now he was voluntarily walking away from the only happiness he'd ever known.

He had to leave while he still could. He had to get away. Had to kill Schuyler if he ever intended to have peace. Doing away with the terrorist was the only way out. It was either Schuyler or him, and all the odds were with the other man.

Zane opened the truck door and was ready to climb into the cab when Lesley appeared on the porch. She walked over to the white column and leaned against it as though needing its support.

He hesitated, his hand on the steering wheel.

Neither moved.

Then, with a sob, his wife rushed down the stairs and raced across the yard.

Zane caught her around the waist and hauled her into his arms. His body absorbed her sobs. He closed his eyes and clung to her.

"Kill the son of a bitch," she whispered.

"I will," he promised.

"Then come home to me."

His throat constricted. As much as he wanted to Zane couldn't make that promise.

* * *

Carl felt he was probably making another one of those colossal mistakes that had marked his relationship with Candy Hoffman. But he had nowhere else to turn.

He parked outside her house and sat in the pickup. Her house was dark, but then, what did he expect at four o'clock in the morning?

Given a choice, he would have opted for someone else, but the only other woman he knew and trusted was Martha Applegate, and he didn't think she'd be up to the task.

There was no help for it. He needed Candy.

With a deep sigh of resignation, he climbed out of the cab and approached the house. It'd been five weeks since he'd last seen her. She seemed to be avoiding him with the same fervor.

Five long, torturous weeks. He wasn't fool enough to admit he hadn't missed her. Thoughts of her consumed his soul. Even now he worried about her and the baby, but there wasn't a damn thing he could do. She'd rejected him, rejected his proposal.

The temptation to turn around and leave was strong. Before he could entertain the notion further, he leaned against the doorbell and waited.

Every likelihood existed that Candy was involved with someone else by now. He tried not to think about that possibility, but he wasn't fool enough not to recognize that she was an attractive woman. Since she'd started dressing like a woman, other men were bound to notice her.

He pressed the doorbell a second time, and silently counted to ten before he released the button.

His heart was heavy, and contacting Candy like this did little to lighten his load.

The porch light went on and he blinked against the sudden brightness.

"What do you want?" Candy shouted through the closed door.

"I need you," he shouted gruffly.

"I'm sure one of your female friends from the Watering Hole would serve just as well."

So she'd been keeping tabs on him. A hint of a smile touched his lips. He'd been so damn busy working on his place that he rarely went out these days. In the past five weeks, he'd probably drank two beers at the local tavern. A couple of friendly women had let it be known that they wouldn't be opposed to a little fun. The sad part of it all was that neither one had tempted him. There'd been a time when Carl would have gladly partaken of their offer. He suspected Candy was to blame for that, as well. Another reason on the growing list of why he shouldn't have come to her now.

"I need your help," he amended. "Just open the door, would you?" He swore under his breath. Patience had never been his strongest trait, and dealing with the most obstinate woman in a three-state radius wasn't helping him any.

"My help?" She opened the door, and stood on the other side of the locked screen door.

Carl thought he was prepared for this but he was wrong. Dead wrong. She was so damned pretty with her hair all mussed, and her robe tightly cinched at her waist. He couldn't see any evidence of the baby yet.

He'd missed her. He hadn't realized how much until just this moment. The temptation to pull her into his arms was so strong that he nearly crushed his hat between his hands.

"It's four in the morning," she chastised, regarding him warily.

"I know," he returned gruffly. "This couldn't wait."

"What is it?"

"I need you to come with me when I talk to Lesley Ackerman."

"Zane's wife?"

He nodded. "She's going to need a woman. I'm not going to be much help."

"What's wrong?"

He resisted the urge to wipe a hand down his face. When he spoke, the words came hard, working their way up his parched throat. "I just got word. Zane's dead. I need you to help me tell his wife."

Chapter Twelve

Lesley knew the precise moment Zane had died. She woke from a deep sleep and an incredible sadness settled over her. Sitting up in bed, she stared into the thick darkness as the realization her husband was dead assaulted her. She wasn't sure how she knew. She just knew.

The grief made her feel as though she were drowning. Her lungs couldn't get enough oxygen. Her broken heart ached. The flood of pain was more than she could bear. Cradling her abdomen to protect her child, she moaned and rocked and softly wept.

In retrospect she was certain what happened next must have been her imagination. An emotional means of dealing with such intense pain. Perhaps it was all wishful thinking. She had no name to give it so she accepted it as a gift. A rare and precious gift.

In the darkness, when her heart felt as if it would burst with grief, Zane came to her. She didn't see him. Not with her eyes. She felt his presence as keenly as if he were standing next to her. The scent of him was everywhere. He was close, so close, she felt his fingers lightly trail down the side of her face.

His love for her and their child filled the room, adding a glow that couldn't be attributed to any light. The words weren't spoken aloud, but she heard them as clearly as if they had been verbalized.

He told her how sorry he was. How desperately he'd wanted to live so he could come back to her and their daughter. He asked her to find it in her heart to forgive him for ever having left her.

Then soon, so much sooner than she wanted, Zane was gone. He left before he could answer her questions, before she could say all the things that crowded her heart.

Suddenly, without warning, the room grew cold and dark once again.

Lesley curled into a tight ball, wrapping his love around her and their baby as tightly as she could, and waited.

Twenty-eight hours later Carl arrived with Candy Hoffman to tell her what she already knew. Both seemed surprised by how well Lesley received the news that Zane was gone.

How gentle Carl had been. His and Candy's tender concern touched her heart. Lesley was grateful for the way Candy sat by her side and held her hand. But it was Candy Hoffman who wept, not Lesley. It was Candy who asked a long list of questions. Candy who demanded answers.

Not Lesley. Not then.

Lesley sat and listened stoically. The words barely penetrated the dense fog of her grief. The details weren't important. In time she'd ask Carl and learn what she needed to know. All that her heart could bear, all that her mind could assimilate in those first few weeks was the confirmation that Zane had been killed.

The months passed. One day tumbled into the next with her barely aware of time passing. She had no appetite. She slept only when her physical body caved in to the demand for rest.

She took a leave of absence from her job, and faced each day with bleak loneliness. She alternated between loving and missing Zane to the point of insanity, to swearing she hated him for the way he'd used and left her. An emotional medium had yet to be found.

The one surprise in all this was the friendship she struck with Candy Hoffman. With Carl, too, but on a different level.

Those first few weeks, Candy made a number of excuses to stop off at the house to visit Lesley. With Mrs. Applegate's encouragement, her newfound friend forced Lesley out of the dark library, urged her to stand and soak up the sunlight. Encouraged her to talk about Zane.

The progress was slow, but eventually Lesley began to look forward to Candy's visits. If for nothing else, Lesley would forever be grateful that Candy helped her take her eyes off her loss enough to recognize the one truly amazing gift Zane had given her: their child.

Because Candy was pregnant and alone, because the new lives their bodies nurtured thrilled them, they shared a deep and abiding bond.

Carl, whom Lesley had always considered brusque and impatient, displayed another side of his personality with her. He made a point of checking up on her often and helped her in numerous ways.

The leaves on the huge maple trees turned several shades of autumn. Burnt orange, gold and bronze leaves covered the yard. The days were much cooler now. The nights longer.

By some unspoken agreement, Carl never stopped off at the house when Candy was there. It amazed Lesley how adept they were at missing one another. She never asked either one about their relationship, or lack of one. But even in her grief, Lesley couldn't help notice how much in love Candy and Carl were.

One afternoon, when the sun shone and the day was crisp and cold, Lesley sat at her favorite spot on the concrete bench where she could view the water. She sat here often, enjoyed breathing in the fresh air. Enjoyed talking to her unborn child.

Over the past several months, Lesley had made friends with Eddie and Dennis, the two young boys Zane had found on the beach that one summer's day. They sometimes came and fed apples to Arabesque, Zane's gelding. Lesley was sure it wasn't her company they found stimulating, but the goodies Mrs. Applegate took delight in feeding them afterward.

Lesley's thoughts were occupied with the boys' visit when she made her way back toward the house. Her musings were interrupted by the sight of Carl's truck barreling down the driveway.

Lesley waited for him.

"Hello, Carl."

"Lesley." He eyed her rounding tummy. Unable to button several pairs of pants now, she'd taken to wearing ones with stretch waistbands. The smock was new and cheerful.

Lesley laughed and pressed her hands over her abdomen. "I'm starting to show, aren't I?"

"You're five months?"

She nodded.

"Candy?"

Lesley understood the question without him having to voice it. "Our due dates are within a week of one another."

He looked away as though he were embarrassed to be asking her about Candy. "How's she feeling?"

"Wonderful, or so she says. I'm teaching her to knit."

One side of his mouth eased up as if the thought amused him.

"She's making a baby blanket," Lesley elaborated.

Once again his gaze avoided hers, but she could tell that his interest was keen. "Is the blanket blue or pink? They can tell the sex of the baby beforehand, can't they?"

Lesley nodded. "The baby's blanket is both pink and blue."

Carl's eyes shot to hers, and widened with disbelief. "Twins. She's having twins?"

"No." Lesley didn't mean to laugh, but she couldn't stop herself. "Since she doesn't know the sex of the baby, she's knitting the blanket in a variety of pastel colors, which include pink and blue."

"Oh."

Lesley swore Carl sounded downright disappointed.

Together they strolled toward the house. "I didn't come to talk to you about Candy."

"Good." The way Lesley figured it, if Carl had something to say to her friend, he should do it himself.

"How are you feeling?" he asked.

They entered the house and Lesley escorted him into the library. It was her favorite room, as it had been for Zane. She spent as much time as she could there. She'd had the attic transformed into one large office. The panoramic view from the office took her breath away. She'd had a number of windows added and loved the way the light filled the room as she worked.

Almost before they even sat down, Mrs. Applegate brought them coffee and a plate of Carl's favorite cookies.

Carl helped himself to a chocolate-chip cookie while Lesley poured. "I brought some papers over for you to look at," Carl said. "It's about the investments we made in that mutual fund group last month. I think you'll be pleased."

Carl had recommended the investment, and after she'd read up on the group herself, Lesley had invested several thousand dollars. She handed Zane's friend a mug and poured her own.

"I'm ready," she announced as she sat down. She wasn't sure what prompted the statement, but she knew it to be true. "Tell me what happened with Zane."

Until that moment she couldn't bear knowing the details, and had blocked everything from her mind. Zane was dead and that was all that was important.

Carl studied her as if to gauge her emotional strength.

"You're sure?"

Lesley assured him that she was.

"Schuyler was holed up in the Middle East."

Lesley knew this much. The country was a tiny one she'd never heard of until the day Carl had arrived with Candy.

"He knew Zane was coming. Any element of surprise had long since been taken away. Knowing that, Zane phoned and invited Schuyler to meet him face-to-face."

How like her husband to confront his enemy. Her chest tightened, knowing Zane had probably walked into a trap, one that had cost him his life.

"Why did Schuyler agree?" Knowing what little she did of the terrorist, Lesley could think of no reason for him to elude Zane, or go back into hiding. According to what Carl had told her, Schuyler was an expert at disguise. He could easily change his appearance enough to have slipped away without a trace.

Carl hesitated, and his gaze held hers. "Zane's plan was brilliant."

Seeing that her husband was dead, Lesley questioned that, but said nothing.

"He had been searching for Schuyler for months, but he did it in an ingenious way. Instead of hiring detectives and paying off informants, he had Schuyler's picture printed on boxes of candy and on matchbooks. He promised a large reward to whoever located him. Then he attacked Schuyler on an entirely different level, as well." The sparkle in Carl's eyes revealed his admiration.

Lesley wasn't sure what he meant.

"Zane went after Schuyler's power base. He had the advantage because Schuyler assumed the explosion had killed Zane. It wasn't until this summer that Schuyler learned otherwise. All the while Zane was building up his strength, he was able to gather vital information."

Lesley shook her head. "I don't understand."

"A man like Schuyler can't operate without money, connections and other means of support. With the help of tracers, Zane managed to filter false information about Schuyler to his supporters. Dissention broke out among the fanatics who backed him, and he was forced to come out of hiding to personally meet with them."

Lesley wasn't sure she entirely understood everything Carl explained, but enough to follow the gist.

"Schuyler made one small mistake that literally cost him millions." Carl smiled as he spoke. "Exactly how Zane managed this I'll never know, but he discovered a bank in the Cayman Islands where Schuyler held several million dollars, unbeknownst to his ardent supporters."

"In other words, the terrorist had cheated his friends."

"Exactly."

"Not only did Zane leak the information, but he got the account number and withdrew almost all the money."

Lesley's gaze fell on the financial papers Carl had brought over for her to read.

"It's not what you're thinking. He took that money and divvied it up to a number of charities."

How like Zane to see that ill-gotten gains would be put to use serving mankind.

"Now you can understand why Schuyler was so eager to meet with Zane," Carl concluded.

"Of course," she whispered. "Schuyler hated him."

Carl's eyes sobered. "Schuyler wanted revenge."

And he'd gotten it, Lesley noted.

"But how did he learn Zane was the one responsible for what was happening with his finances?"

"I'm not sure, but once that information was out, Zane had no choice but to deal with Schuyler himself. The options had been taken away from him. His greatest fear was that the terrorist would come after you. He had to make sure that would never happen."

"The meeting," Lesley prompted, wanting to know everything. Where once knowing the details of Zane's death had been a burden too heavy to carry, now she found the information vital. She hungered for every tidbit Carl could give her.

"Zane suggested they meet in the desert."

Naturally her husband would do whatever he could to protect innocent bystanders, although the anonymity of a crowd would have protected him. "Surely he didn't go in there alone."

"No. But then neither did Schuyler."

Zane had knowingly walked into a meeting, with a man who had powerful reasons to hate him, and a burning desire to kill him.

"I don't know exactly what did happen, I don't think anyone ever will," Carl said, his face grim and tight. "But when it was over, there were no witnesses and Schuyler was dead."

"You're sure of that?"

"Very. It was more than revenge, Lesley. Dan and Dave's death wasn't the only thing this was about. The world's a better place without Schuyler."

And an emptier, lonely place without Zane, Lesley added mentally.

She pressed her palms against her abdomen. "I needed to know... I thought the baby should hear the details herself when the time came for me to tell her about her father."

"Her?" Carl eyed her skeptically.

"I don't know for certain yet, but that's what I believe." It was what Zane had told her the night he'd come to her, but she didn't explain that to Carl.

They sat and drank the remainder of their coffee in silence. Lesley's thoughts were filled with the sacrifice Zane had made and what his final moments must have been like. She was confident that his last moments on this earth were filled with thoughts of her.

Carl seemed wrapped up in his own deep musings. "I understand you and Candy are seeing the same gynecologist," her friend said casually.

"Dr. Wilson."

He reached for a cookie and broke it in half as though he suspected Mrs. Applegate had hidden something of value inside. "Is everything alright with the pregnancy?"

"So far, so good. Why don't you ask her yourself?"

The suggestion hung in the air between them like a helium-filled balloon. He seemed to consider the suggestion, then sadly shook his head. "If she needs anything... tell her she can count on me."

"I'm not Western Union, Carl." She couldn't allow herself to become involved with what was happening between these two people she loved. She wanted to help, and tried to be gentle, seeing that Carl had been so kind and patient with her. "If you don't want to tell her these things yourself, write her a letter.''

His eyes briefly lit up at the suggestion, but she watched as the frustration and discouragement clouded his judgment. ''I've already said everything. She knows I'd help her in any way she needed, but she's just too damn stubborn to ask.''

Candy, stubborn! It was almost more than Lesley could do not to suggest that Carl take a look in the mirror himself.

Thanksgiving Day, Candy woke feeling melancholy and fat. She was nearly six months pregnant and there wasn't a single pair of jeans that fit her any longer. Lesley had opted to buy maternity pants a month earlier, but Candy had held out until that very morning.

It didn't help any that she would be spending the day alone. Lesley was joining her parents, something Candy had suggested herself. Now she wished she hadn't been quite so encouraging.

Lesley Ackerman had turned out to be one of the best friends Candy had ever had. Other than the obvious, the two shared a good deal in common.

Never once had Lesley drilled her over her relationship with Carl. Never once had she tried to patch matters up between the two of them. Never once had she offered her advice. For all three, Candy was grateful. Nothing anyone said would convince her to marry Carl Saks. Nothing.

Candy dressed and dragged herself into the kitchen wearing her slippers. The bouts of morning sickness had long since passed, replaced with a healthy appetite. She'd been careful about weight gain and was well within the parameters Dr. Wilson had suggested.

Maintaining her diet during the holidays couldn't be any more difficult than abstaining from caffeine. How she missed her morning cup of leaded fuel. If Carl knew...

She paused midthought, unwilling to allow her mind to dwell on the subject of Carl Saks. Not this day when she was already feeling abandoned and lonely. Not today when families all across the country gathered together to count their blessings.

Candy had several blessings, but no family. If ever there was a day to treat herself, it was this one. After a meager breakfast and equally dinky lunch, Candy dressed in one of her new outfits and drove to Bluebeard's, the restaurant where Carl had taken her for their first official date. It seemed far more trouble than it was worth to roast a turkey and all the trimmings for just one person.

The crowded parking lot wasn't encouraging, but Candy eventually found a spot and hurried inside out of the cold. The weather had dipped below freezing and the sky was dark. The weatherman had suggested snow, and that suited her just fine. In an effort to lift her spirits, she'd decided to decorate for Christmas that evening.

A hostess Candy didn't recognize greeted her with a warm holiday welcome. Several people crowded around the cash register and the woman wrote everyone's name down on a waiting list.

"A table for one," Candy said when it came her turn to give her name. "How long is the wait?" She was already hungry and the smells coming from the dining room were delicious.

"Forty-five minutes, I'm afraid."

"Oh." That long. It was difficult to hide her disappointment. She should have thought to make reservations.

"There's another party here whose name is about to come up that also asked for a table for one. Perhaps you two would be willing to share?"

"It's fine with me, if the other party doesn't object" What a lovely solution, Candy mused, delighted with the suggestion. She hadn't been that keen on eating alone and would welcome the company.

"I'll be right back," the woman told her. She returned a moment later. "That will be fine. Follow me."

Candy's mistake was that she didn't stop to look at her dinner companion until they reached the table. When she turned to thank the person who'd been willing to have her join him, her eyes collided with Carl Saks's brooding gaze.

Her first inclination was to call back the hostess and tell her she'd had a change of heart, but the restaurant was packed. It was exactly the type of behavior what Carl would expect of her.

"Thank you," she said, making sure her voice revealed none of her feelings. She pulled out the chair and sat down. If he objected, then he could be the one to leave. Squatter's rights must hold for something!

Candy must have studied the menu for five straight minutes while she gathered her composure. The busboy delivered water, bread and soft butter before she set the menu aside. There'd never been any question of what she wanted to order. Turkey and all the trimmings.

Carl looked as if he'd rather be anyplace on this earth than sitting across the table from her. His brow was knit and he couldn't seem to take his brooding eyes off her.

"You're wearing maternity clothes," he muttered when she forcefully returned his intense gaze.

He probably hadn't recognized her. That was the only explanation she could think of why he'd agreed to this awkwardness.

A cheerful waitress swung by their table to take their order. Her good spirits must have rubbed off on Carl because he was smiling when the waitress left. His grin slowly faded as his eyes met Candy's.

This was going to be difficult. Candy smoothed the napkin onto her lap.

"Perhaps we should agree to put aside our differences for this one dinner," Carl suggested. "We got along well enough before."

It would have been childish to disagree. "All right," she said with obvious reluctance. To her way of thinking, the less they had to say to each other the better.

"You look real pretty, Candy."

Her gaze shot back to his. She didn't want to believe him because to do so would make her vulnerable again and she couldn't allow that to happen. Not again. "Thank you." She put as little feeling into the words as possible.

"How are you feeling?"

"Wonderful."

An uneasy silence followed. Much more of this stilted awkwardness and her appetite would be ruined. Their waitress, delivering their salads, interrupted it. Both seemed eager to pick up the conversation when she left.

"How's the ranch coming along?" she asked.

"Can you feel the baby move yet?" he asked at precisely the same moment.

Candy hesitated, not sure who should answer first. Carl gestured toward her.

"The baby kicks and stretches all the time. Generally he waits until I'm in bed and comfortable before he decides to twist and shout."

"He?" His grin was wide and eager.

Leave it to Carl to pick up on that. "I never have been able to think of the baby as an *it*. He is a generic term. I could just as easily be having a girl."

"Lesley says you've taking up knitting."

Candy was uncomfortable with the thought of her friend talking about her with Carl. Lesley only mentioned Carl in passing, and that was just the way Candy preferred it.

"I didn't know that Lesley discussed my business with anyone." Candy knew she sounded priggish, but she was disappointed that the woman she considered her friend had shared this bit of information with Carl.

"I asked about you," Carl admitted grudgingly. "I don't want you to think Lesley spoke out of turn. There were several items I wanted her to relay to you, but she was quick to tell me she isn't Western Union." His grin was sheepish, and Candy was sure he'd rather she not know that. His willingness to admit this impressed her.

"What kind of things?" Human nature being what it is, Candy was curious.

"I wanted to be sure you had everything you needed."

"I do," she whispered. "Thank you for paying the doctor and the hospital bills in advance." She had only learned that at her last doctor's appointment.

He shrugged as though to say it was only fair that he do so.

Their waitress stopped at their table. "Is something wrong with the salad?"

"No," Candy was quick to assure her.

"Take your time, but I thought you'd want to know your dinner's almost up."

For being hungry only moments earlier, Candy had nearly forgotten the dinner salad. She raised her right hand from her lap and reached for her fork.

Carl froze, his narrowed gaze appeared to he studying her hand. "You're wearing the ring."

A sinking feeling settled in the pit of Candy's stomach. She'd forgotten all about the diamond ring. The one Carl had literally tossed her on his way out the door.

"You'll note it's on my right hand." This was said with authority as though it made a real difference.

"Your right hand," Carl repeated.

"You did give it to me," she added defensively.

"Yes," he mumbled, "but I thought you'd take it back to the jeweler's. I assumed you had."

"No." She dipped the fork into the salad with unnecessary force. "It's a lovely diamond." The minute she tasted the first bite, Candy realized she wasn't going to be able to continue this charade. It had seemed like a simple matter at first, to join Carl for dinner. They were both civilized people, but this had proved to be so much more difficult than she would have thought.

"Why the right hand?" he quizzed.

She didn't answer him until she had a chance to build up her bravado. She knew the defensiveness was back in her voice, but it was necessary. "I couldn't very well put it on my left hand, could I?"

A muscle tightened in his jaw. "No. But why wear it at all?"

"If you want it back, fine." She started to slip it off her finger, but he stopped her.

"I said the ring was yours to do with as you like. I'm just surprised that you chose to wear it."

She reached for her fork, determined to eat every last shred of lettuce on her plate even if she had to choke it down. "As I said earlier, it's a beautiful ring." Which was a gross understatement. The solitaire diamond was the most beautiful piece of jewelry she owned, but that wasn't the reason she put it on her finger. He could have mounted a piece of rock salt and she would have worn it with pride had he truly loved her.

Carl seemed intent on downing his salad, as well.

"I...I..." She started and stopped, then purposely looked past him. Her voice was small when she was able to continue. "I know you proposed because I was pregnant, not because of any feelings for me. When you insisted I keep it, I tried putting it away, but I found myself slipping it on and off my finger and pretending we were engaged. One day I decided just to keep it on because I felt closer to you while wearing the ring."

Carl leaned forward, his elbows braced against the table. "Say that first part again. You're confusing me."

''What part?''

''The point about me proposing because you were pregnant.''

''Yes?'' She didn't understand what he questioned.

His patience seemed to be wearing thin. ''Answer me this. Do you or do you not love me?'' He was beginning to sound short tempered.

Candy didn't so much as blink. ''Only an idiot would think I didn't love you, Carl Saks.''

Her response appeared to fuel his displeasure with her. ''Then might I ask why you rejected my proposal?''

''Because you don't love me.''

''Like hell I don't.'' He slammed his fist against the tabletop, causing what remained of their salad to leap halfway off the plate. Water sloshed onto the white linen tablecloth. The entire restaurant stopped talking and stared at them before resuming conversation.

She glared at him, leaned even farther toward him and whispered between clenched teeth, ''Then why did you, with your own words, tell me that the only reason you were proposing was because I was pregnant?''

''Because you were—you are!''

''Did it ever occur to you that a woman needs to be wanted and loved for herself? I certainly don't want to be accused of trapping you into marriage. If you'd asked me to be your wife and once, just once, so much as mentioned the word *love,* I would have leapt into your arms and wept for joy.''

He stared at her as if she were speaking a foreign language. The waitress hurried to their table, removed the salad plates and delivered their entrées.

Candy dug into her turkey and dressing as though she didn't plan on eating for the next month. She damn near choked on every bite, but she'd do that rather than let Carl know how badly he'd hurt her.

Her mouth was full of mashed potatoes and giblet gravy when Carl carefully set his napkin on top of the table. He stood, walked around to her side and got down on one knee.

Candy was so shocked, she couldn't swallow.

"I have never loved a woman as much as I do you, Candy Hoffman. You're stubborn, beautiful and about the most obstinate woman I've ever known. I made a mistake earlier, and I don't intend to repeat it."

Stunned, she stared at him.

"Will you marry me?" he asked softly, his love shining through his eyes.

Candy's hand shook as she reached for the water glass. She managed to down half of it before she could speak. Even then she found the words wouldn't make it past the huge lump in her throat.

"I love our baby, too, in case you have any doubt. I can't help thinking he's going to be hell on wheels."

Candy started to laugh and cry at the same time. She wrapped her arms around Carl's neck and buried her face in his shoulder. He loved her. He honestly loved her.

Carl kissed the side of her face. "I take it that was a yes. If not, it's too damn bad. I'm not taking no for an answer this time."

With his arms wrapped around her waist, he stood and twirled around.

Candy threw back her head and laughed with joy. This had to be the happiest day of her life.

Chapter Thirteen

"Hello, boy." Lesley carefully approached Zane's gelding, Arabesque. The Arabian's sleek black neck appeared over the stall door, anticipating a treat. He tossed his mane and snorted when she hid an apple behind her back, telling her he was well aware of her games.

"Something tells me I've spoiled you," she teased, holding out the apple in the palm of her hand. Like her, Arabesque missed Zane. His temper had been fierce in the first weeks after Zane's death, almost as if he were aware of what had happened to his master.

Even now, after months of building a friendship, the exquisite Arabian barely tolerated Lesley's presence and only then because she brought him a treat.

Even Eddie and Dennis hadn't made much progress with Arabesque. Buttercup, the filly, patiently stood still and allowed the two boys to groom her, but not Arabesque.

"You miss him, don't you, boy?" Lesley asked as she stroked the gelding's long, smooth neck. Arabesque nudged her shoulder and bobbed his head.

"Me, too," she whispered brokenly. She didn't know what was wrong with her lately. Perhaps it was the pregnancy that made her so weepy of late. Or the news of Candy and Carl's engagement. The two had set their wedding for New Year's Eve and Candy had asked that Lesley stand up as her maid of honor. She was both honored and delighted.

Lesley certainly didn't begrudge the couple their happiness, but their joy seemed to magnify her loneliness, her loss, her unhappiness.

The baby stirred within her womb, and without thinking, Lesley pressed her palm against her stomach, wondering at the sudden movement.

Arabesque jerked his head in an upward motion and whinnied loudly.

The softest of sounds drifted to her from the barn door. A ready smile touched her lips as she turned to greet the newcomer.

It was then that she saw Zane.

Her breath stopped and her heart quickened as she struggled to mentally deal with what her eyes were telling her.

It wasn't him. The man who stood just inside the shadow-filled barn bore no scars. He was devoid of the ugly, red marks that scored her dead husband's face. This man was thin. Terribly, terribly thin.

It was Zane. It had to be.

She must be dreaming, Lesley decided. Missing Zane as much as she did, her fertile mind had conjured up his image. But if this was a dream, Lesley never wanted to wake.

Neither spoke, but then Lesley wondered if words were possible between them. Although he seemed solid and real, it wouldn't have surprised her had he vanished.

He took two steps toward her. The limp was there, and each measured footfall appeared to bring him pain. Still, he kept his gaze trained on her as if making the pain-filled trek to her was his goal. The love in his eyes all but blinded her.

"Zane," she said in a soft, almost voiceless breath, afraid if she spoke he'd disappear, afraid words would drive him away. Slowly, her fingers trembling, she reached out and touched his cheek with the lightest of contact. His skin was warm and soft and his eyes drifted closed as if he had waited his entire life for this moment. As if her gentle touch had broken an evil spell that held him prisoner.

"Zane?" she repeated again.

He captured her hand and held it firmly against his face.

He felt real. Alive. His chest rose and fell with each breath. His heart beat. She saw with her own eyes the way a vein hammered in his neck.

All at once Lesley started to shake. Tears choked her throat and she tried to take in what was happening. Confusion swamped her. After taking months to accept that her husband was dead, she discovered he was very much alive.

"Say something," she pleaded, fighting back the sobs. "Let me know you're real."

He brought her into his arms then, his hold so powerful and tight, he nearly knocked the breath from her lungs. His hands were in her hair as he repeatedly whispered, "I'm alive. Until this moment. Until I touched you, I was dead. I love you, Lesley, with all my heart, with all my being."

His words confused her even more, but his touch . . . his touch was familiar and intimate. And welcome, so very welcome.

He kissed her with a hunger that wouldn't be satisfied with one kiss or a thousand. A hunger a lifetime couldn't quench. Again and again his mouth claimed hers, cherished her, loved her, using his lips and tongue, his breath, all that he was.

"How . . . ? Not possible . . ." she pleaded as she inched her mouth from his. She needed answers. Needed to understand how it was possible for him to have stayed away from her all these months and allow her to believe he was dead.

Zane led her back into the house, his steps slow and measured. Mrs. Applegate stood in the kitchen, weeping with happiness.

"He took ten years off my life, he did, showing up this way," she announced to Lesley.

Lesley's own shock hadn't been any less dramatic. But if that was the price, then Lesley gladly surrendered each one of those years for the opportunity to have her husband back.

"How is it possible?" she asked again, needing answers, afraid to believe until she had them.

Zane led her into the library and lowered her into the leather wingback chair. He sat on the ottoman in front of her and reached for her hands, gripping them in his own, his hold painfully tight. Lesley didn't care; she needed the pain to reinforce that this was really happening.

"I arranged to meet Schuyler in the desert," he began, his face grim and tight with the memory. "We weren't there more than five minutes when all hell broke loose. Schuyler was as intent on killing me as I was in making sure he went straight to hell."

Lesley bit her lower lip, which trembled uncontrollably. "He's dead?"

"Yes. I shot him, and saw the hate fill his eyes before he died. I heard him curse me as he screamed in pain. I wasn't the only one who wished him dead, and some of my friends have their own way of dealing with the bodies of their enemies.

"I made one mistake," Zane whispered, and kissed her fingers. "Schuyler had made a contingency to kill me if I succeeded in killing him first. He planted a bomb."

Lesley gasped. Not another explosion. Zane had barely survived the first one.

"The world caved in on me and that was all I knew until I woke in a French hospital."

"French?"

"I have no recollection of how I got there, and had no clue who I was or where I was when I woke. It's taken me six months to regain my memory."

"But you died," she insisted, remembering the night his spirit had come to her, had filled their bedroom and told her goodbye. "I felt it. I woke up and you were there...."

His clear dark eyes held hers, unable to conceal his shock. "That was real?" He shook his head as though he wasn't sure this was possible. "When I first felt the blast I remember thinking that I wasn't going to make it. That escape now would be impossible. All I could think about was you and the baby."

"You came to me."

"Yes. I don't know how it is possible, but I remember those few, precious moments with you. And I remember the pain, fighting it as best I could, choosing the physical agony over the summons of the intense white light.

"Week after week I lay in the hospital, more dead than alive. All I knew was that it was important that I live. Sometimes I would dream of a woman's love, but those dreams were veiled and I woke frustrated and angry."

"Your face?" She traced her fingertips down his smooth skin.

"The doctors seemed to think repairing my face would jolt my memory. It didn't work."

She kissed the edge of his mouth and braced her forehead against his. "You're...beautiful." She could find no other word to describe the difference. She'd always guessed that he'd been an attractive man, but nothing like this. He was the epitome of every woman's dream.

"Not as beautiful as you are, pregnant with our child." He planted his hands on her swollen abdomen, lifted her top and kissed her bare belly.

"Six months, Zane." She wept with frustration. "You've been gone six months."

"I know." The bleak sadness in his eyes told her he begrudged every one of those days apart from her.

"It wasn't only amnesia," he told her, and she couldn't doubt his desolate state. "I was in a coma for nearly a week. The doctors told me I suffered a stroke during that time, which isn't uncommon. When I did wake, one side was briefly paralyzed. Not only was my memory gone, but my condition was complicated with other problems. It's a miracle I'm here." At her soft gasp, he kissed her fingertips. "I've recovered, and I'm here with you. That's all that matters. Everything else is in the past."

"Oh, Zane."

"All the time I was in a mental haze, I felt this burning sense of urgency. A number of times, the pain and the frustration were more than I could bear and I wished for death, but I never entertained those thoughts long. Somehow I knew it was critical I live. Week after hopeless week I faced an empty future."

"What triggered your memory?" Whatever it was, she would be forever grateful.

A hint of a smile touched his eyes. "An infant's cry. I don't know how many times I'd walked the hospital corridors. I'll never know what prompted me to visit the maternity floor. Perhaps my inner spirit sensed my need to view life from the beginning.

"After so much time, I welcomed a new start. I remember wishing I could be born again. As I stood looking at the newborn infants, one let out a deep piercing scream.

"All at once, your face—your beautiful, perfect face—came to me. The memory was so brief, I shouted with agony, willing it back. The black veil lifted and eventually everything came back in bits and spurts."

He smiled and gently kissed her. "The look, the love, the excitement expressed in your face when you told me you were pregnant glowed from your eyes. In that briefest of moments, I remembered."

All these lonely months he'd been in a strange hospital, wrestling nameless demons, struggling to regain his memory and his sanity.

"Don't leave me again," she pleaded with him, struggling with her tears. "I couldn't go through this again." Even as she choked out the words, she knew his own hell had been much worse than hers. Zane fought to live, but didn't know for whom or why.

"Never again," he promised, kissing her.

"You're alive, alive," she chanted, wanting to shout with joy. The beauty of that reality filled her heart and crowded her soul.

As soon as it was possible, they made love. Zane's hands stroked her breasts, then rested on her rounded stomach. Their child moved against him and his eyes widened as his gaze slowly traveled to her.

"A girl," she whispered.

"Dr. Wilson told you?"

"No," she told him with a happy, satisfied smile. "You did."

His look was skeptical.

"I thought you had," she amended, and brought his mouth down to hers. "If we have a boy, then all I can say is that we'll have to try again."

Her husband's dark eyes sparkled. "Anything you say, sweetheart."

* * * * *

Silhouette®

S P E C I A L   E D I T I O N™

COMING NEXT MONTH

#1009 THE COWBOY AND HIS BABY—Sherryl Woods
That's My Baby!/And Baby Makes Three
Forgetting Melissa Horton had never been easy for Cody Adams.
And now that he'd discovered she was the mother of his baby, he
had even more reason to reconcile with his one true love....

#1010 THE MAN, THE MOON AND THE
MARRIAGE VOW—Christine Rimmer
The Jones Gang
Evie Jones had been waiting all her life for love to conquer all.
Single father Erik Riggins had given up on love, but once he'd
laid eyes on Evie, nothing would stop him from proposing matrimony!

#1011 FRIENDS, LOVERS...AND BABIES!—Joan Elliott Pickart
The Baby Bet
Ryan MacAllister and Deedee Hamilton never expected that their
status as friends would change to lovers. But then Deedee's pregnancy
changed all the rules--and Ryan had to face his true feelings for her....

#1012 BUCHANAN'S BRIDE—Pamela Toth
Buckles & Broncos
She was just what he needed, but tall, silent cowboy Taylor Buchanan
would never let his guard down around Ashley Gray. It was up to
Ashley to lasso his heart and show him how to love again....

#1013 CHILD OF MIDNIGHT—Sharon De Vita
If renegade cop Michael Tyler had a soft spot, it was for kids in trouble.
This time the child came complete with hotshot Alexandria Kent—the
one woman who set his heart on fire and whom he'd sworn he'd stay
away from.... ·

#1014 THE WEDDING CONTRACT—Kelly Jamison
If Laura Halstead accepted Jake McClennon's generous offer of
marriage, she could keep custody of her daughter. While Jake stressed
a union in name only, Laura was hoping this marriage of convenience
would be interrupted by love....

Bestselling author

RACHEL LEE

takes her Conard County series to new heights with

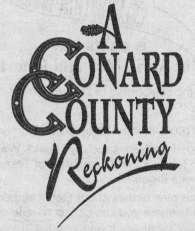

A CONARD COUNTY Reckoning

This March, Rachel Lee brings readers a brand-new, longer-length, out-of-series title featuring the characters from her successful Conard County miniseries.

Janet Tate and Abel Pierce have both been betrayed and carry deep, bitter memories. Brought together by great passion, they must learn to trust again.

"Conard County is a wonderful place to visit! Rachel Lee has crafted warm, enchanting stories. These are wonderful books to curl up with and read. I highly recommend them."
    —*New York Times* bestselling author
        Heather Graham Pozzessere

Available in March, wherever Silhouette books are sold.